英美经典诗歌选译

陈楚娃◎选译

安徽师范大学出版社
ANHUI NORMAL UNIVERSITY PRESS
·芜湖·

图书在版编目(CIP)数据

英美经典诗歌选译 / 陈楚娃选译. —芜湖:安徽师范大学出版社,2021.12
ISBN 978-7-5676-5337-5

Ⅰ.①英… Ⅱ.①陈… Ⅲ.①诗集—英国②诗集—美国 Ⅳ.①I12

中国版本图书馆CIP数据核字(2021)第273333号

英美经典诗歌选译

陈楚娃◎选译

责任编辑:汪碧颖　责任校对:辛新新
装帧设计:丁奕奕　责任印制:桑国磊
出版发行:安徽师范大学出版社
　　　　　芜湖市北京东路1号安徽师范大学赭山校区
网　　址:http://www.ahnupress.com
发 行 部:0553-3883578　5910327　5910310(传真)
印　　刷:苏州市古得堡数码印刷有限公司
版　　次:2021年12月第1版
印　　次:2021年12月第1次印刷
规　　格:700 mm × 1000 mm　1/16
印　　张:18.5
字　　数:293千字
书　　号:ISBN 978-7-5676-5337-5
定　　价:66.00元

凡发现图书有质量问题,请与我社联系(联系电话:0553-5910315)

前 言

诗歌凝聚着人类理性之光与美好情感，也是语言精华、智慧结晶。诗歌是人类精神文化的一个闪光点，古今中外，概莫能外。东西方国家都有自己的诗歌文化，风格各异，源远流长。它似一束束熊熊火炬在人类历史长河中熠熠生辉，照亮了世世代代人的生存、奋进之路。

纵观几千年人类文明发展史，尽管物换星移，风云变幻，世界五大洲精英诗人真实地勾勒了绵绵悠长的历史画卷，为各个时代谱写了万世流芳的华美诗章，他们唱出了时代最强音。无论什么诗歌流派，或现实主义，或浪漫主义，或魔幻主义；无论什么风格，或朦胧幽晦，或自由奔放，或蕴含哲理、讽喻幽默等，无不反映了诗家对历代不同时期社会的心灵体察和人生感悟，对当时政治、文化、经济、民生诸方面的精辟之剖析。

“诗言志”。诗人文思泉涌、妙笔生花，其主题、灵感及创作激情根植于现实生活之沃土，来源于创造社会财富的广大劳苦大众之命运与疾苦。正如中国伟大诗人屈原有着忧国忧民之情怀，“长太息以掩涕兮，哀民生之多艰”，他才能谱写出光照人寰的不朽诗篇。正因为屈原具有关切人民的思想感情、浪漫而丰盈的想象力、炉火纯青之思辨以及精湛之诗艺，才能将灵感创作推向极致的巅峰。

我两次孑然一身地漫游了欧洲60天，从而深刻地体会到东西方文化的底蕴都是那么博大精深，不可思议。当我登上雪花飞舞的阿尔卑斯山时，当我漫游瑞士伯尔尼绿树葱茏的阿尔河谷时，当我在法国静静流淌的赛纳河河畔徜徉时，当我站在伦敦桥上观赏海鸥凌空飞翔时，我不由得浮想联翩，回想起锦瑟年华所读过的欧洲文化大师的诗章及小说。细思量，中外诗艺各有千秋，相映成辉，光照日月。

我造访了英国戏剧家莎士比亚的家乡。这位十五六世纪文艺复兴的代表人物——在书桌前写下了反映社会生活缩影的旷世杰作，在人生舞台上寻找自我灵感和素材。我还造访了浪漫主义诗歌的先驱——华兹华斯的鸽屋（Dove Cottage）。我沿着他家附近的山谷前行，一路上山光水色，令人流连忘返。过去，诗人常在此漫步、徘徊，领略大自然对其情操之陶冶。我恍然大悟：难怪乎，他的诗《黄水仙》写得那么具有空灵美！他的诗情画意在人间仙界的大湖区找到灵感。难怪乎，这位“湖畔诗人”在波光潋滟的湖水中洗濯了诗笔，其诗风清雅而又淡泊，并体现了“人之心灵元素带有大自然精神色调”的美学思想。

在欧洲七国，我一路畅游了20多个城市，感悟良多。我想从英国的明媚风光中捎给莘莘学子和英美诗歌爱好者一瓣心香、一朵野花、一枚鹅卵石、一掬清冽之湖水……，它恰似一股清雅而又浪漫的诗风徐徐吹来。因此，我选译了100首英美经典诗歌，以飨读者。诚请广大读者能赐教一二，不胜感激！

选译者：陈楚娃

于黄海之滨假日港湾

2019年7月

目　录

Contents

英国诗歌

They Flee from Me

Thomas Wyatt

They flee from me that sometime did me seek
With naked foot, stalking in my chamber.
I have seen them gentle, tame and meek
That now are wild and do not remember
That sometime they put themselves in danger
To take bread at my hand; and now they range,
Busily seeking with a continual change.

Thanked be fortune, it hath been otherwise
Twenty times better; but once in special,
In thin array after a pleasant guise,
When her loose gown from her shoulders did fall,
And she me caught in her arms long and small;
Therewithal sweetly did me kiss,
And softly said, *Dear heart, how like you this?*

It was no dream, I lay broad waking.
But all is turned thorough my gentleness
Into a strange fashion of forsaking;
And I have leave to go of her goodness
And she also to use newfangleness.
But since that I so kindly am served,
I would fain know what she hath deserved.

他们从我身边逃离

托马斯·韦艾特

他们从我身边逃离，有时，
　我寻觅，在屋里赤足潜行。
他们温文尔雅，而又驯良；
　现在却是野性，而忘却：
　有时他们使自身处于危险，
从我手里取面包。他们忙于
安排寻求一种持续之变革。

感谢上苍命运，尚有其他
　二十次更好。这次却特殊，
她愉悦装束后，瘦衣紧身。
　当松弛睡衣从她肩头落下，
　她用细长的双臂抱住我。
因此，我甜蜜地亲吻着，
轻声说：亲爱的，怎这样？

这不是梦，我平躺着而醒来。
　我的温柔之情彻底毁了，
转为一种怪异的抛弃方式。
　她心地善良，而我必离去；
　她也要弄着新奇之花样。
既然我如此仁慈地受到宽待，
我欣然告慰，她会有好报应。

Sonnet

Michael Drayton

Since there's no help, come, let us kiss and part—
Nay, I have done: you get no more of me;
And I am glad, yea, glad with all my heart
That thus so cleanly I myself can free.
Shake hands forever, cancel all our vows,
And when we meet at any time again,
Be it not seen in either of our brows
That we one jot of former love retain.
Now at the last gasp of love's latest breath,
When, his pulse failing, Passion speechless lies,
When Faith is kneeling by his bed of death,
And Innocence is closing up his eyes,—
Now, if thou wouldst, when all have given him over,
From death to life thou mightst him yet recover.

商籁诗

迈克尔·德莱顿

既然无望，哦！让我们吻别——
不，我完了：你不再拥有我。
我愉悦！是的，全身心愉悦，
这么彻底地能够自我解脱了。
握手永别吧！抛弃一切誓约；
无论何时，我们再一次相逢，
彼此额头上，再也寻找不见：
以往爱情保留的那一丝痕迹。
“爱情”，最后已经奄奄一息，
脉搏衰竭，“激情”无言撒谎；
“信仰”在其临终榻前而跪下。
“天真”正闭合着闪烁之明眸——
哦！倘若你甘愿赠予他一切，
或许，让其生命起死回生吧！

Sonnets(1–3)

William Shakespeare

(1)

My mistress' eyes are nothing like the sun;
Coral is far more red than her lips' red:
If snow be white, why then her breasts are dun;
If hairs be wires, black wires grow on her head,
I have seen roses damasked, red and white,
But no such roses see I in her cheeks;
And in some perfumes is there more delight
Then in the breath that from my mistress reeks.
I love to hear her speak, yet well I know
That music hath a far more pleasing sound:
I grant I never saw a goddess go;
My mistress, when she walks, treads on the ground.
  And yet by heaven, I think my love as rare,
  As any she belied with false compare.

(2)

When to the sessions of sweet silent thought,
I summon up remembrance of things past,
I sigh the lack of many a thing I sought,
And with old woes new wail my dear time's waste:
Then can I drown an eye (unus'd to flow)
For precious friends hid in death's dateless night,
And weep a fresh love's long since cancelled woe,
And moan th'expense of many a vanished sight.

商籁诗三首

威廉·莎士比亚

(1)

我情妇的明眸怎比上太阳，
珊瑚远比其樱唇更红艳；
若雪白莹，为何乳房暗褐？
若发如丝，而其乌发如云。
我曾经见红白玫瑰织锦缎，
却未见鲜花绽放于其面颊；
她身上香气袭人，喘息中，
飘逸更为令人愉悦之芳香。
我爱听娇嗔声，却深知晓：
音乐会鸣奏更悦耳的旋律。
我断言：从未见女神走过，
而情妇轻踩着地面上漫步。
　对天发誓，我想珍奇之爱，
　犹如她不符合虚假之比拟。

(2)

何时我能甜美地静静思索，
以唤起如烟往事之回忆；
悲叹匮乏那苦苦追寻之事，
新哀旧怨荒废宝贵之时光。
我既不回眸（也不可流盼），
挚友隐匿于无尽死亡黑夜；
哭泣新爱，久已消失悲愁，
哀叹失去几许流逝之美景。

Then can I grieve at grievances foregone,
And heavily from woe to woe tell o'er.
The sad account of sore-bemoaned moan,
Which I new pay as if not pay'd before.
  But if the while I think on thee (dear friend)
  All losses are restor'd， and sorrows end.

(3)

When in disgrace with Fortune and men's eyes,
I all alone beweep my outcast state,
And trouble deaf heaven with my bootless cries,
And look upon my self and curse my fate.
Wishing me like to one more rich in hope,
Featur'd like him, like him with friends possessed,
Desiring this man's art, and that man's scope,
With what I most enjoy contented least;
Yet in these thoughts my self almost despising,
Happily I think on thee, and then my state,
(Like to the Lark at break of day arising)
From sullen earth sings hymns at Heaven's gate,
  For thy sweet love remembered such wealth brings,
  That then I scorn to change my state with Kings.

我唯忧伤以往逝去之忧伤，
诉说重重苦恼，而又苦恼。
痛苦之呻吟，呻吟之悲述，
新近奉献如往昔未曾付出。
　若我思念啊！（亲爱的挚友），
　一切损失挽回，悲情结束。

（3）

我遭命运、世人白眼羞辱，
我孑然哭泣流离之境遇；
烦怨苍天聋哑、跣足号啕，
顾影自怜，诅咒时乖命蹇。
希冀着成为前程远大之人，
如其人特征，而高朋满座；
向往此人才艺，彼人视野，
我唯能享有，即少许满足。
我几乎是轻蔑着自身思想，
颇兴味思虑你及个人境况；
（好似云雀破晓时而腾起），
从阴沉大地咏唱天堂圣歌。
　因汝爱意，忆及捎至财富，
　我轻蔑与帝王去交换地位。

Fear No More the Heat o' the Sun

William Shakespeare

Fear no more the heat o' the sun,
  Nor the furious winter's rages.
Thou thy worldly task hast done,
  Home art gone and ta'en thy wages.
Golden lads and girls all must,
As chimney-sweepers, come to dust.

Fear no more the frown of the great,
  Thou art past the tyrant's stroke.
Care no more to clothe and eat,
  To thee the reed is as the oak.
The sceptre, learning, physic, must
All follow this and come to dust.

Fear no more the lightning flash,
  Nor the all-dreaded thunder-stone.
Fear not slander, censure rash.
  Thou hast finished joy and moan.
All lovers young, all lovers must
Consign to thee and come to dust.

No exorcisor harm thee,
  Nor no witchcraft charm thee.
Ghost unlaid forbear thee.
  Nothing ill come near thee.
Quiet consummation have,
And renownèd be thy grave.

骄阳炙热，不再恐惧

威廉·莎士比亚

骄阳炙热，不再恐惧，
　冬雪肆虐，也不怕。
汝已完成尘世之劳作，
　家园远去且获薪酬。
金色少年如扫烟囱人，
都必将渐渐化为尘埃。

权贵蹙眉，不再恐惧，
　暴君鞭笞也能承受。
不再有衣食之忧，
　君认为芦苇似橡树。
权杖、学识、医术，
必随此类渐化为尘埃。

电闪雷鸣，不再恐惧，
　雷石，毫不畏缩。
诽谤、苛评，不害怕，
　君已饱尝悲欢离合。
年轻情侣交付于汝，
都必将渐渐化为尘埃。

妖魔对汝，难以伤害，
　巫术，不能困惑。
解索之幽灵，且容忍，
　无一病恙殃及君。
尽善尽美，乃至极致，
而墓碑，名声且远扬。

The Good-Morrow

John Donne

I wonder by my troth, what thou, and I
Did, till we loved? Were we not weaned till then,
But sucked on country pleasures, childishly?
Or snorted we in the seven sleepers' den?
'Twas so; but this, all pleasures fancies be.
If ever any beauty I did see,
Which I desired, and got, 'twas but a dream of thee.

And now good morrow to our waking souls,
Which watch not one another out of fear;
For love, all love of other sights controls,
And makes one little room, an every where.
Let sea-discoverers to new worlds have gone,
Let maps to other, worlds on worlds have shown,
Let us possess one world, each hath one, and is one.

My face in thine eye, thine in mine appears,
And true plain hearts do in the faces rest,
Where can we find two better hemispheres
Without sharp north, without declining west?
Whatever dies, was not mixed equally;
If our two loves be one, or, thou and I
Love so alike that none do slacken, none can die.

美好翌日

约翰 · 多恩

我奇怪所发的誓言，我与你啊！
　直至相爱做何事？不放弃，
仅孩子气似吮吸着乡村乐趣？
　或在七人卧室里鼾声大作？
如此而已，却想象为无穷乐趣。
若我真的看见任何美妙之处，
那么，愿望或获得，即是梦见你。

此时，美好翌日唤醒爱之灵魂，
　彼此不再害怕注视着对方；
因爱情，节制其他景观之爱，
　每一处，皆营造几许小空间。
让新世界大海探索者，远去吧！
让地图向世人展示不同之寰宇，
让我们拥有一个世界又互相拥有。

彼此脸颊，映照在对方瞳孔里，
　真诚而朴素之心显现于面容，
那里，能否发现两个更好半球？
　无酷寒北方，无衰落西方。
无论如何死亡，却不混为一谈。
若你与我之间爱情心心相印，
爱情如此相像：不松弛，不消亡。

The Anniversary

John Donne

All Kings, and all their favourites,
All glory of honours, beauties, wits,
The sun itself, which makes times, as they pass,
Is elder by a year, now, then it was
When thou and I first one another saw:
All other things, to their destruction draw,
Only our love hath no decay;
This, no tomorrow hath, nor yesterday,
Running it never runs from us away,
But truly keeps his first, last, everlasting day.

Two graves must hide thine and my corpse,
If one might, death were no divorce,
Alas, as well as other Princes, we
(Who Prince enough in one another be,)
Must leave at last in death, these eyes, and ears,
Oft fed with true oaths, and with sweet salt tears;
But souls where nothing dwells but love;
(All other thoughts being inmates) then shall prove
This, or a love increased there above,
When bodies to their graves, souls from their graves remove.

And then we shall be thoroughly blessed,
But now no more, then all the rest.
Here upon earth, we're Kings, and none but we.

周年纪念日

约翰·多恩

　所有国王，以及其宠幸者，
　所有辉煌、荣光、美与智，
太阳本身即创造时代；一切
皆经过岁月沧桑。而在此时，
你与我，彼此初次才相识。
其他事物，也相继近乎毁灭，
　唯有我们爱情才不会衰微。
这样既无明天，也无昨天，
时间迅跑，它永不远离而去，
珍藏着由始至终的永恒日子。

　两墓穴必然隐匿彼此遗体；
　若有力量，死后也不分离。
哎呀呀！吾侪以及其他王公
必定最终死亡；（凡王公者，
足以接踵而入）。在视听觉上，
常注入真正誓言、甜涩之泪。
　灵魂，除了爱情无处可居；
（一切思想同栖），遂将证明：
一切爱在天堂上与日俱增，
遗体尚在坟墓里，灵魂超度。

　那时，彼此至诚地祝福吧！
如今不会；随之，一切安息。
大地上，吾辈是国王，除此，

Can be such Kings, nor of such subjects be;
Who is so safe as we? where none can do
Treason to us, except one of us two.
  True and false fears let us refrain,
Let us love nobly, and live, and add again
Years and years unto years, till we attain
To write threescore this is the second of our reign.

无人堪称王者或臣属。谁能
比你我安全？那里也无一人，
胆敢反叛，除了彼此中一位。
　真与假唯恐吾侪自我克制，
高尚地爱吧！活着而繁衍；
年年岁岁直至获得，并书写：
六十春秋，即吾侪第二王朝。

My Silks and Fine Array

William Blake

My silks and fine array,
My smiles and languish'd air,
By love are driv'n away;
And mournful lean Despair
Brings me yew to deck my grave:
Such end true lovers have.

His face is fair as heav'n
When springing buds unfold
O why to him was't giv'n
Whose heart is wintry cold?
His breast is love's all worship'd tomb,
Where all love's pilgrims come.

Bring me an axe and spade,
Bring me a winding sheet;
When I my graves have made,
Let winds and tempests beat:
Then down I'll lie as cold as clay.
True love doth pass away!

我的丝衣与华丽服饰

威廉·布莱克

我的丝衣与华丽服饰，
爱之微笑、痛苦之表情，
哀伤而又憔悴之绝望，
将是永远地烟消云散了。
捎来紫衫以饰我墓穴：
真正恋人，皆有此结局。

当春天花蕾绽放之时，
他脸庞似天空一般明朗。
哦！为何不赋予其人：
那颗冷如冰霜之心呢？
其胸膛，爱之敬仰者
之墓，所有朝圣者光临。

捎于我一把斧头和铲子，
捎于我一块裹尸布吧。
当我打造好自己的墓穴，
让狂风暴雨骤起吧：
我将似一抔冻土而卧下。
真爱确实一去不复返了！

The Lamb

William Blake

Little Lamb, who made thee?
Dost thou know who made thee?
Gave thee life, and bid thee feed,
By the stream and o'er the mead;
Gave thee clothing of delight,
Softest clothing, wooly, bright;
Gave thee such a tender voice?
Making all the vales rejoice?
Little Lamb, who made thee?
Dost thou know who made thee?

Little Lamb, I'll tell thee,
Little Lamb, I'll tell thee:
He is called by thy name,
For he calls himself a Lamb.
He is meek, and he is mild;
He became a little child.
I a child, and thou a lamb,
We are called by his name.
Little Lamb, God bless thee!
Little Lamb, God bless thee!

小羊羔

威廉 · 布莱克

小羊羔，谁创造了你？
你晓得，谁创造了你？
赐予你生命，吩咐你
去小溪边、草场吃草；
赐予你华美之羊绒衣，
它那么柔和而又光亮。
赐予你娇嫩的声音，
让所有溪谷充斥欢乐？
小羊羔，谁创造了你？
你晓得，谁创造了你？

小羊羔，我将告诉你，
小羊羔，我将告诉你：
他以你的名字而命名，
因他自称为：小羊羔。
他既温顺，而又和善；
他成为一个小小婴孩。
我是孩子，你是羊羔，
我们都以“他”命名。
小羊羔，上帝祝福你！
小羊羔，上帝祝福你！

My Love Is Like a Red, Red Rose

Robert Burns

I

O, my love is like a red, red rose,
  That's newly sprung in June.
O, my love is like the melody,
  That's sweetly play'd in tune.

II

As fair art thou, my bonnie lass,
  So deep in love am I,
And I will love thee still, my dear,
  Till a' the seas gang dry.

III

Till a' the seas gang dry, my dear,
  And the rocks melt wi' the sun!
And I will love thee still, my dear,
While the sands o' life shall run.

IV

And fare thee weel, my only love,
  And fare thee weel a while!
And I will come again, my love,
  Tho' it were ten thousand mile!

我的恋人像红玫瑰

罗伯特 · 彭斯

I

哦！我的恋人像红玫瑰，
　新近开于六月。
哦！我的恋人像那旋律，
　甜美地弹在曲里。

II

美丽少女，多么艳丽！
　我深深地爱你；
亲爱的，我永远爱你，
　直至海水枯干。

III

亲爱的，直至海水枯干，
　石头熔于太阳下！
亲爱的，我永远爱你，
　而生命沙粒将尽。

IV

再见吧！我唯一恋人，
　一时辰再相见！
亲爱的，我将会归来，
　穿越了千山万水！

Sonnet

William Wordsworth

The world is too much with us; late and soon,
Getting and spending, we lay waste our powers:
Little we see in Nature that is ours;
We have given our hearts away, a sordid boon!
This Sea that bares her bosom to the moon;
The winds that will be howling at all hours,
And are up-gathered now like sleeping flowers;
For this, for every thing, we are out of tune;
It moves us not. —Great God! I'd rather be
A Pagan suckled in a creed outworn;
So might I, standing on this pleasant lea,
Have glimpses that would make me less forlorn;
Have sight of Proteus rising from the sea;
Or hear old Triton blow his wreathèd horn.

商籁诗

威廉·华兹华斯

世界非能应付；或早或迟，
获得又消耗，或浪费能量：
无疑，自然界少许属人类。
吾侪全心奉献，自私而实惠！
大海面对月亮敞开着胸怀。
狂风，何时都在大声号啕，
此时，采集似入眠之花卉。
由于这一切，吾侪失了调；
并非感动——上帝！吾宁
做吮吸过时信条之异教徒；
或许，伫立于愉悦之牧地，
瞥见景物，却又少许寂寞；
观赏普罗透斯[①]从海面升起，
或聆听老特里顿[②]吹奏螺号。

注：①普罗透斯：希腊神话中变幻无常的海神。
②特里顿：希腊神话中半人半鱼的海神。

Lucy Gray

William Wordsworth

Oft I had heard of Lucy Gray:
And when I cross'd the wild,
I chanced to see at break of day
The solitary child.

No mate, no comrade Lucy knew;
She dwelt on a wide moor,
The sweetest thing that ever grew
Beside a human door!

You yet may spy the fawn at play,
The hare upon the green;
But the sweet face of Lucy Gray
Will never more be seen.

'To-night will be a stormy night—
You to the town must go;
And take a lantern, Child, to light
Your mother through the snow.'

'That, Father! will I gladly do:
'Tis scarcely afternoon—
The minster-clock has just struck two,
And yonder is the moon!'

露西 · 格雷

威廉 · 华兹华斯

我常听说露西姑娘。
我穿越荒野之时，
碰巧见东方刚破晓，
这个孤苦的孩子。

她无情人也无友伴，
居住在空旷沼地。
最美之事曾发生于：
此家人的房门旁！

你会发现小鹿玩耍，
野兔穿行绿草地；
而露西姣美之容貌，
再也无人去欣赏。

“今晚将是暴风夜——
你必须去那城里；
孩子，提灯笼照亮：
你母亲走过雪地。”

“爹！我高兴做这事，
现在，还不到下午——
教堂钟声正敲两下，
那边即一轮月亮！”

At this the Father raised his hook,
And snapp'd a faggot-band;
He plied his work;— and Lucy took
The lantern in her hand.

Not blither is the mountain roe:
With many a wanton stroke
Her feet disperse the powdery snow,
That rises up like smoke.

The storm came on before its time:
She wander'd up and down;
And many a hill did Lucy climb:
But never reach'd the town.

The wretched parents all that night
Went shouting far and wide;
But there was neither sound nor sight
To serve them for a guide.

At day-break on a hill they stood
That overlook'd the moor;
And thence they saw the bridge of wood
A furlong from their door.

They wept—and, turning homeward,cried
'In heaven we all shall meet!'
—When in the snow the mother spied
The print of Lucy's feet.

此时父亲举起镰刀，
突然折断了柴捆；
他正使劲地劳作着——
露西手提着灯笼。

山上小鹿也不快活：
露西随意地踩踏，
脚步驱散粉状雪花，
似烟尘一般飞扬。

暴风已提前来临了，
她在崎岖路上迷失；
露西，翻山又越岭，
但未能抵达城里。

通宵夜，可怜父母，
旷野上远近呼喊；
寂然无声，无景物
作为他们的向导。

拂晓父母站在山岗，
俯视着一片沼地；
那里，却看见木桥，
离家门一弗朗远。

父母返家——哭喊：
“让我们天堂见！”
在雪地，母亲探出：
露西踩着的脚印。

Then downwards from the steep hill's edge,
They track'd the footmarks small;
And through the broken hawthorn hedge,
And by the long stone-wall:

And then an open field they cross'd:
The marks were still the same;
They track'd them on, nor ever lost;
And to the bridge they came:

They follow'd from the snowy bank
Those footmarks, one by one,
Into the middle of the plank;
And further there were none!

—Yet some maintain that to this day
She is a living child;
That you may see sweet Lucy Gray
Upon the lonesome wild.

O'er rough and smooth she trips along,
and never looks behind;
And sings a solitary song
That whistles in the wind.

从陡峭山崖往下走，
追踪着小脚印；
穿越破裂山楂树篱，
在长长的石墙边。

他们穿越开阔田野，
仍是同样标记；
踩着脚印未走迷失，
随后，来到桥边；

从雪岸边一直跟踪：
这脚印，一步步，
走进那块厚板中间。
两边，视野茫茫！

而此山脉延续至今，
她是活着的孩子；
你会见姣美之露西，
走在孤寂荒野上。

坎坷或平坦，她独
前行，从不回望；
唱着一支孤凄歌谣，
歌声在风中呼啸。

We Are Seven

William Wordsworth

A simple child, dear brother Jim,
That lightly draws its breath,
And feels its life in every limb,
What should it know of death?

I met a little cottage girl,
She was eight years old, she said;
Her hair was thick with many a curl
That cluster'd round her head.

She had a rustic, woodland air,
And she was wildly clad;
Her eyes were fair, and very fair,
—Her beauty made me glad.

'Sisters and brothers, little maid,
'How many may you be?'
'How many? seven in all, 'she said.
'And wondering looked at me.

'And where are they? I pray you tell,'
She answered, 'Seven are we,
'And two of us at Conway dwell,
'And two are gone to sea.

我们是七个

威廉·华兹华斯

淳朴的好兄弟杰姆，
他在轻轻呼吸着；
每一肢体跳动生命，
他怎么了解死亡？

我遇见一农家女孩，
她说，已八岁了。
一绺绺浓密的卷发，
簇拥脑袋儿四周。

她带有林地人纯朴，
也颇有粗野土气；
明亮大眼尤为秀美——
她的美赏心悦目。

我问:“小姑娘，有
多少兄弟姐妹?”
“多少？总共七个。”
她迷惑地瞧我。

“请告诉他们在哪里?”
她回答:“七个。
其中两人居住康维，
两人去了大海边。

‘Two of us in the church-yard lie,
‘My sister and my brother,
‘And in the church-yard cottage, I
‘Dwell near them with my mother.’

‘You say that two at Conway dwell,
‘And two are gone to sea,
‘Yet you are seven; I pray you tell
‘Sweet Maid, how this may be?’

Then did the little Maid reply,
‘Seven boys and girls are we;
‘Two of us in the church-yard lie,
‘Beneath the church-yard tree.’

‘You run about, my little Maid,
‘Your limbs they are alive;
‘If two are in the church-yard laid,
‘Then ye are only five.’

‘Their graves are green, they may be seen,’
The little Maid replied,
‘Twelve steps or more from my mother’s door,
‘And they are side by side.

‘My stockings there I often knit,
‘My 'kerchief there I hem;
‘And there upon the ground I sit—
‘I sit and sing to them.

姐姐和兄弟静静地，
卧在教堂墓地里；
妈和我住墓地农舍，
就在他们附近。”

“你说，两人住康维，
两人去了大海边。
而你们七人，请说，
可爱女孩，怎可能？”

随后，小女孩回答：
“七个男女娃子，
两人躺在教堂墓地，
在那棵大树底下。”

“你四圈跑，小女孩
四肢十分灵巧；
若两人躺在墓地里，
你们只是五个。”

“青绿墓地可见他们，”
小女孩回答道：
“妈妈房门前十多步，
他们并排地卧着。

那里，我经常织袜，
缝着小手帕边；
我还坐那处地面上，——
为他们唱着歌儿。

'And often after sunset, Sir.
'When it is light and fair,
'I take my little porringer,
'And eat my supper there.

'The first that died was sister Jane;
'In bed she moaning lay,
'Till God released her of her pain,
'And then she went away.

'So in the church-yard she was laid,
'And all the summer was dry,
'Together round her grave we played,
'My brother John and I.

'And when the ground was white with snow,
'And I could run and slide,
'My brother John was forced to go,
'And he lies by her side,'

'How many are you then,' said I,
'If they two are in Heaven?'
'The little Maiden did reply,
'O Master! we are seven.'

'But they are dead; those two are dead!
'Their spirits are in heaven!'
'Twas throwing words away; for still
The little Maid would have her will,
And said, 'Nay, we are seven!'

先生，日落西山后，
天色发亮，真美啊！
我常端着小浅碗儿，
坐在那里吃晚饭。

首先，珍妮去世了；
她卧床呻吟着，
直至上帝解脱痛苦，
她才撒手而去。

因此，她躺在墓地；
整个夏季干燥，
我们却在那里玩耍，
我和兄弟约翰。

当大地白雪皑皑时，
我能跑步或滑雪；
而约翰被迫地走了，
他卧于珍妮身边。”

我问：“若他俩还在
天堂，多少人?”
小女孩确实回答道：
“哦，先生，七个。”

“他俩死了，死了！
而灵魂升上天堂！”
这话说错吗？然而，
小女孩却固执己见：
“不，我们七个！”

Abou Ben Adhem

Leigh Hunt

Abou Ben Adhem (may his tribe increase!)
Awoke one night from a deep dream of peace,
And saw, within the moonlight in his room,
Making it rich, and like a lily in bloom,
An angel writing in a book of gold: —
Exceeding peace had made Ben Adhem bold,
And to the presence in the room he said,
'What writest thou?' The vision raised its head,
And with a look made of all sweet accord,
Answer'd 'The names of those who love the Lord.'
'And is mine one?' said Abou. 'Nay, not so,'
Replied the angel. Abou spoke more low,
But cheerly still; and said, 'I pray thee then,
Write me as one that loves his fellow-men.'

The angel wrote, and vanished. The next night
It came again with a great wakening light,
And show'd the names whom love of God had bles'ed,
And lo! Ben Adhem's name led all the rest.

阿布·本·艾德姆

利·亨特

本·艾德姆（愿其种族兴旺！）
夜间，他从宁静之深梦醒来，
月光辉映房间，而富丽堂皇，
宛如百合花绽放。他只见有
一天使正在黄金册书写着：——
忒祥和之氛围，令阿布壮胆。
他对房间出现的影子而说道:
“你写什么?”幻影抬起头，
并带有慈祥而又从容的表情，
他回答：“爱上帝之人名。”
阿布问：“有我名字?”“没”，
天使答。阿布声音更低沉了，
他高兴地说道：“为你祈祷!”
且写：“我作为爱同胞之人。”

天使写完遂消失。翌日之夜，
令人惊醒之强光照了进来，
显示福佑：“爱上帝之人名”；
瞧吧！艾德姆却是名列榜首。

So We'll Go No More a Roving

George Byron

So, we'll go no more a roving
  So late into the night,
Though the heart still be as loving,
  And the moon still be as bright.

For the sword outwears its sheath,
  And the soul outwears the breast,
And the heart must pause to breathe,
  And Love itself have rest.

Though the night was made for loving,
  And the day returns too soon,
Yet we'll go no more a roving
  By the light of the moon.

我们将不再漫游

乔治·拜伦

而我们将不再漫游
　太迟直至深夜；
心灵仍旧一往情深，
　月光皎洁如初。

因刀剑已拔出其鞘，
　胸内灵魂疲惫；
心脏必然停止呼吸，
　爱神本身休憩。

良宵美景为爱而设，
　白昼匆匆来临；
而我们将不再漫游，
　在明亮月光下。

I Am

John Clare

1

I am — yet what I am， none cares of knows;
My friends forsake me like a memory lost: —
I am the self-consumer of my woes; —
They rise and vanish in oblivious host,
Like shadows in love's frenzied stifled throes: —
And yet I am, and live— like vapours tossed.

2

Into the nothingness of scorn and noise, —
Into the living sea of waking dreams,
Where there is neither sense of life or joys,
But the vast shipwreck of my life's esteems;
Even the dearest, that I love the best
Are strange—nay, rather stranger than the rest.

3

I long for scenes, where man hath never trod
A place where woman never smiled or wept
There to abide with my Creator, God;
And sleep as I in childhood, sweetly slept,
Untroubling, and untroubled where I lie,
The grass below— above the vaulted sky.

我 是

约翰·克莱尔

1
我是什么？——无人在乎知晓，
　友人抛弃我，似乎缺失记忆——
我是一个悲哀的自我憔悴者；——
　其升起、消失在大量忘却中，
像热恋之阴影，窒息又阵痛——
我还是，活着——像水汽升起，

2
进入那轻蔑、噪音的虚空之中——
　进入梦境醒来之生存大海。
那里缺乏活力和快乐的感觉，
　仅有我生命尊严的巨大沉船，
甚至最亲爱之人，至爱之人，
　也生疏——不，比他人更生疏。

3
我向往之景观，男人从未践踏，
　那里女人从不嬉笑或哭泣，
那里人人遵从造物主：上帝。
　我似在孩提时代里甜蜜睡熟，
无忧无虑，卧于那处无人干扰；
下方草地——头顶上穹窿苍天。

Sonnet — to Sleep

John Keats

O soft embalmer of the still midnight,
Shutting, with careful fingers and benign,
Our gloom-pleas'd eyes, embower'd from the light,
Enshaded in forgetfulness divine:
O soothest Sleep! If so it please thee, close
In midst of this thine hymn my willing eyes,
Or wait the 'Amen,' ere thy poppy throws
Around my bed its lulling charities.
Then save me, or the passed day will shine
Upon my pillow, breeding many woes,—
Save me from curious Conscience, that still lords
Its strength for darkness, burrowing like a mole;
Turn the key deftly in the oiled wards,
And seal the hushed Casket of my scoul.

商籁诗——致睡眠

约翰·济慈

哦，静寂子夜轻涂香膏者，
　以仁慈手指小心翼翼闭合——
我们忧郁惬意之目光避开：
　凉亭之光，掩于忘怀圣境。
多么甜美梦乡！若你愉悦，
　在此圣歌中，我乐意合眼，
等待“阿门”声；将罂粟
　撒于灵床四周，中断慈悲。
拯救我！逝去白昼将辉映
于枕上，引起一阵阵哀伤——
　我良心渴望救赎，它仍为
黑暗之主宰力，似鼹掘洞；
　在润油锁孔灵巧地旋钥匙，
封闭了我灵魂里静谧之棺材。

La Belle Dame Sans Merci

John Keats

I

Ah, what can ail thee, wretched wight,
   Alone and palely loitering;
The sedge is wither'd from the lake,
   And no birds sing.

II

Ah, what can ail thee, wretched wight,
   So haggard and so woe-begone?
The squirrel's granary is full,
   And the harvest's done.

III

I see a lilly on thy brow,
   With anguish moist and fever dew;
And on thy cheek a fading rose
   Fast withereth too.

IV

I met a lady in the meads
   Full beautiful, a faery's child;
Her hair was long, her foot was light,
   And her eyes were wild.

V

I set her on my pacing steed,

无情的美女

约翰·济慈

I

啊！可怜人为何苦恼？
　苍白、独自踯躅；
湖边，蓑衣草枯萎了，
　也无鸟雀儿啼鸣。

II

啊！可怜人为何苦恼？
　枯槁而又忧愁；
松鼠谷仓已填塞满了，
　庄稼也收割完毕。

III

我瞧百合簪于你额头，
　露珠湿热又悲苦；
你面颊上残淡之玫瑰，
　正迅疾地枯萎了。

IV

我在草地相遇一少女，
　犹仙子美艳之极；
长长发束，步履轻盈，
　明眸里透着野性。

V

我让她骑上踱步的马，

And nothing else saw all day long;
For sideways would she lean, and sing
A faery's song.

VI

I made a garland for her head,
And bracelets too, and fragrant zone;
She look'd at me as she did love,
And made sweet moan.

VII

She found me roots of relish sweet,
And honey wild, and manna dew;
And sure in language strange she said,
I love thee true.

VIII

She took me to her elfin grot,
And there she gaz'd and sighed deep,
And there I shut her wild sad eyes—
So kiss'd to sleep.

IX

And there we slumber'd on the moss,
And there I dream'd, ah woe betide,
The latest dream I ever dream'd
On the cold hill side.

X

I saw pale kings, and princes too,

　一整天什么不见；
她总倚着路边，唱着
　一支仙境之曲。

VI
我编织花环戴其头上，
　另有手镯、香腰带；
她脉脉含情地凝视我，
　并发出甜蜜叹息。

VII
她为我寻见甜味之根、
　野生蜂蜜与甘露；
她说，却以奇怪语言：
　我真心地爱上你。

VIII
她领我至精灵洞穴里，
　凝望着而深叹息；
我闭合其野性之泪眼，
　深吻着乃至入眠。

IX
我们沉睡在青苔之上，
　我梦里降临悲情；
梦境尾声，我曾梦见：
　在寒冷的山陵边。

X
我见苍白国王和王子，

Pale warriors, death-pale were they all;
Who cry'd— 'La belle Dame sans merci
Hath thee in thrall!'

XI

I saw their starv'd lips in the gloam
With horrid warning gaped wide,
And I awoke, and found me here
On the cold hill side.

XII

And this is why I sojourn here
Alone and palely loitering,
Though the sedge is wither'd from the lake,
And no birds sing.

　苍白武士面若死灰；
他们喊：“无情的美女，
　你陷于奴役之中！”

XI
薄暮中，我见其饿唇
　张大，可怕而警示。
我醒了，发现却处于
　这寒冷的山陵边。

XII
这是我为何逗留于此，
　苍白、独自踯躅；
湖边，蓑衣草枯萎了，
　也无鸟雀儿啼鸣。

Meg Merrilies

John Keats

I

Old Meg she was a Gipsy,
And liv'd upon the Moors;
Her bed it was the brown heath turf,
And her house was out of doors.

II

Her apples were swart blackberries,
Her currants pods o' broom;
Her wine was dew of the wild white rose,
Her book a churchyard tomb.

III

Her Brothers were the craggy hills,
Her Sisters larchen trees—
Alone with her great family
She liv'd as she did please.

IV

No breakfast had she many a morn,
No dinner many a noon,
And 'stead of supper she would stare
Full hard against the Moon.

玛革 · 梅里莉丝

约翰 · 济慈

I

老玛革是个吉卜赛人，
　住在沼泽地上；
其床铺是褐色之草皮，
　屋子在门户外。

II

有毒黑莓、茶麓荚果、
　金银花且作苹果；
白色野玫瑰之露为酒，
　其书即教堂坟墓。

III

嶙峋山陵是她的兄弟，
　落叶松即姐妹——
她与这一大家庭相处，
　生活其乐融融。

IV

许多清晨，她无早点，
　午间也无正餐；
她总狠狠地紧盯月亮，
　以此代替晚餐。

V

But every morn of woodbine fresh
　She made her garlanding,
And every night the dark-glen Yew
　She wove, and she would sing.

VI

And with her fingers old and brown
　She plaited Mats o' Rushes,
And gave them to the Cottagers
　She met among the Bushes.

VII

Old Meg was brave as Margaret Queen
　And tall as Amazon:
An old red blanket cloak she wore;
　A chip hat had she on.
God rest her aged bones somewhere—
　She died full long agone!

V

每天晨曦，她以鲜艳
　忍冬花做着花环；
每晚暗色幽谷之紫杉，
　她边纺，边吟唱。

VI

她以苍老的褐色手指，
　编织灯心草席；
在灌木丛中，她遇见
　农舍人作为礼物。

VII

她勇似玛格丽特女王，
　高似亚马孙族人：
身穿红毛毡的旧大氅，
　头戴着破旧帽子。
上帝让朽骨安息某处——
　她死去早已久远！

I Remember, I Remember

Thomas Hood

I remember, I remember
The house where I was born,
The little window where the sun
Came peeping in at morn;
He never came a wink too soon,
Nor brought too long a day,
But now, I often wish the night
Had borne my breath away!

I remember, I remember
The roses, red and white,
The violets, and the lily-cups,
Those flowers made of light!
The lilacs where the robin built!
And where my brother set
The laburnum on his birth-day, —
The tree is living yet!

I remember, I remember
Where I was used to swing,
And thought the air must rush as fresh
To swallows on the wing;
My spirit flew in feathers then,
That is so heavy now,
And summer pools could hardly cool

我铭记，我铭记

托马斯·胡德

我铭记，我铭记：
我曾诞生之屋；
清晨时，旭日东升，
从小窗隐约初现。
它从未早来片刻，
也未捎来长昼。
如今我常盼望黑夜，
将我的呼吸捎走！

我铭记，我铭记：
红玫瑰，白玫瑰，
紫罗兰与百合花萼，
花朵由光营造！
知更鸟在丁香筑巢。
我兄弟在生日时
那天，植金链花树——
此树仍旧鲜活！

我铭记，我铭记：
那里，我常荡秋千，
想象新鲜空气必然
冲入飞燕之翅膀。
那时灵魂如羽轻扬，
而今，如此沉重！
夏日池塘几乎难以

The fever on my brow!

I remember, I remember
The fir trees dark and high;
I used to think their slender tops
Were close against the sky:
It was a childish ignorance,
But now 'tis little joy
To know I'm farther off from Heaven
Than when I was a boy.

清凉我额头上高热!

我铭记，我铭记:
高耸的茂密杉林;
我常想起颀长树冠,
几近于浩渺苍穹。
虽孩子气的无知啊!
但此时尚有余庆,
我比当时男孩知晓:
尚且离着天堂还远。

Sonnet

Elizabeth Browning

How do I love thee? Let me count the ways.
I love thee to the depth and breadth and height
My soul can reach, when feeling out of sight
For the ends of Being and ideal Grace.
I love thee to the level of everyday's
Most quiet need, by sun and candle-light.
I love thee freely, as men strive for Right;
I love thee purely, as they turn from Praise.
I love thee with the passion put to use
In my old griefs, and with my childhood's faith.
I love thee with a love I seemed to lose
With my lost saints,— I love thee with the breath,
Smiles, tears, of all my life! and, if God choose,
I shall but love thee better after death.

商籁诗

伊丽莎白·布朗宁

如何爱汝？让我计算方式：
我爱汝，深至灵魂所达的
三维度；我感觉茫茫不见：
生存之尽头，理想之优雅。
我爱汝能达日常最需求的——
程度，似璨然阳光与蜡烛。
我自由之爱犹为权力斗争；
纯洁之爱犹唱完那赞美诗。
我爱汝以激情，它曾倾泻
往昔悲伤，且以童年信仰。
我爱汝，似乎以逝去之爱、
逝去圣贤——爱汝以呼吸、
微笑、眼泪、生命！上帝
选择，我将爱汝至死不渝。

A Musical Instrument

Elizabeth Browning

What was he doing, the great god Pan,
   Down in the reeds by the river?
Spreading ruin and scattering ban,
Splashing and paddling with hoofs of a goat,
And breaking the golden lilies afloat
   With the dragon-fly on the river.

He tore out a reed, the great god Pan,
   From the deep cool bed of the river:
The limpid water turbidly ran,
And the broken lilies a-dying lay,
And the dragon-fly had fled away,
   Ere he brought it out of the river.

High on the shore sat the great god Pan
   While turbidly flowed the river;
And hacked and hewed as a great god can,
With his hard bleak steel at the patient reed,
Till there was not a sign of the leaf indeed
   To prove it fresh from the river.

He cut it short, did the great god Pan,
   (How tall it stood in the river!)
Then drew the pith, like the heart of a man,
Steadily from the outside ring,

一种乐器

伊丽莎白·布朗宁

伟大潘神，在小河边、
　低芦苇丛正做什么？
废墟延伸，诅咒播散，
羊蹄蹚水，溅起水花。
金百合花漂浮又折断，
　蜻蜓点水于小河边。

伟大潘神，从凉沁的
　深深河床撕扯芦苇；
清澈水流，湍湍而过，
折裂百合濒死、倒伏。
他将之捎出小河前，
　蜻蜓早已逃之夭夭。

伟大潘神，端坐河边，
　小河水流湍湍而过；
伟大潘神尽力地砍劈，
灰暗利刃切削了硬苇，
直至无一片叶之迹象，
　且证明它鲜亮出水。

伟大潘神，折短芦苇，
　（它在小河立多高!）
遂从芦苇外围，从容
取出男人心状之木髓。

And notched the poor dry empty thing
　In holes, as he sat by the river.

'This is the way, 'laughed the great god Pan
　(Laughed while he sat by the river),
'The only way, since gods began
To make sweet music, they could succeed.'
Then, dropping his mouth to a hole in the reed,
　He blew in power by the river.

Sweet, sweet, sweet, O Pan!
　Piercing sweet by the river!
Blinding sweet, O great god Pan!
The sun on the hill forgot to die,
And the lilies revived, and the dragon-fly
　Came back to dream on the river.

Yet half a beast is the great god Pan,
　To laugh as he sits by the river.
Making a poet out of a man:
The true gods sigh for the cost and pain,—
For the reed which grows nevermore again
　As a reed with the reeds in the river.

当他端坐在小河边时，
　用干燥的空茎刻凹洞。

潘神笑曰："此为妙策。"
　（他坐河边朗朗大笑），
"唯一办法：众神着手，
创造雅乐，即会成功！"
他以口唇对芦苇小洞，
　在小河边魔幻吹奏。

潘神啊！真仙乐贯耳！
　在小河边渗透甜美！
伟大潘神！眩目动听！
山上太阳竟忘却落山。
百合复活，蜻蜓飞回，
　在小河边重返梦乡。

伟大潘神，半神半兽，
　他坐河边朗朗大笑，
从男人中创造出诗人。
真神叹息代价与痛苦——
因芦苇不会再长高，
　它已成小河里苇丛。

I Do Not Love Thee!

Caroline Norton

I do not love thee! —no! I do not love thee!
And yet when thou art absent I am sad;
And envy even the bright blue sky above thee,
Whose quiet stars may see thee and be glad.

I do not love thee! —yet, I know not why,
Whate'er thou dost seems still well done, to me—
And often in my solitude I sigh—
That those I *do* love are not more like thee!

I do not love thee! —yet, when thou art gone
I hate the sound (though those who speak be dear)
Which breaks the lingering echo of the tone
Thy voice of music leaves upon my ear.

I do not love thee! —yet thy speaking eyes,
With their deep, bright, and most expressive blue—
Between me and the midnight heaven arise,
Oftener than any eyes I ever knew.

I *know* I do not love thee! —yet, alas!
Others will scarcely trust my candid heart;
And oft I catch them smiling as they pass,
Because they see me gazing where thou art.

我不爱恋你！

卡罗琳·诺顿

我不爱恋你！——不！不爱！
当你离去时，我却悲伤不已；
甚至嫉妒你头顶上蔚蓝晴空，
而静谧星辰，喜洋洋地张望你。

我不爱恋你！——不知为何？
无论你有何作为，却近乎完美。
我时常在孤独之中，长叹息——
而我真爱之人，并非如同你！

我不爱恋你！——你离去时，
我却讨厌那些人亲昵之话语，
它打断了绵长回响之余声；
你乐感之音仍回荡于我耳边。

我不爱恋你！你会说话眼睛，
深邃而明亮，碧蓝而饱含深情——
升起在我与子夜天堂之间，
比我曾知晓的明眸，更为熟悉。

我知晓：不爱恋你！——唉！
他人几乎不相信我有诚心；
我常见他们走过，莞尔一笑，
因为明白我正凝视：你在哪里。

The Eagle

Alfred Tennyson

He clasps the crag with crooked hands;
Close to the sun in lonely lands,
Ringed with the azure world, he stands.

The wrinkled sea beneath him crawls;
He watches from his mountain walls,
And like a thunderbolt he falls.

鹰

阿尔弗雷德·丁尼生

它以弯曲利爪紧钩着巉岩；
在孤寂荒原上，近于太阳。
它立起，与万里碧空共鸣。

它匍匐下方，大海波浪起伏；
它从山崖峭壁之上俯瞰。
它飞落时，声似雷霆巨响。

Sonnet

Alfred Tennyson

Now sleeps the crimson petal, now the white;
Nor waves the cypress in the palace walk;
Nor winks the gold fin in the porphyry font:
The fire-fly wakens: waken thou with me.
Now droops the milkwhite peacock like a ghost,
And like a ghost she glimmers on to me.
Now lies the Earth all Danae to the stars,
And all thy heart lies open unto me.
Now slides the silent meteor on, and leaves
A shining furrow, as thy thoughts in me.
Now folds the lily all her sweetness up,
And slips into the bosom of the lake:
So fold thyself, my dearest, thou, and slip
Into my bosom and be lost in me.

商籁诗

阿尔弗雷德·丁尼生

此时绛红、白色花瓣入眠，
宫殿路边的柏枝不再摇曳。
斑岩池里金鳍鱼不再眨眼；
萤火虫醒了，唤起你与我。
乳白色孔雀犹如幽灵降临，
她幽魂似地对我微微闪烁。
大地所有达那厄①去星辰；
你的心扉坦荡地向我敞开。
此时静静流星飞驰，留下
闪光痕迹，如你思想铭刻
于我。百合拢住芳馨花香，
悄悄地浸入湖泊胸脯之中。
而亲爱的，你蜷缩着玉体，
滑入我的怀抱，融为一体。

注：①达那厄：古希腊神话中阿尔戈斯国王之女。主神宙斯化作金雨与之相会。后来，她生了一个男孩柏修斯。

Ring Out, Wild Bells

Alfred Tennyson

Ring out, wild bells, to the wild sky,
The flying cloud, the frosty light:
The year is dying in the night;
Ring out, wild bells, and let him die.

Ring out the old, ring in the new,
Ring, happy bells, across the snow:
The year is going, let him go;
Ring out the false, ring in the true.

Ring out the grief that saps the mind,
For those that here we see no more;
Ring out the feud of rich and poor,
Ring in redress to all mankind.

Ring out a slowly dying cause,
And ancient forms of party strife;
Ring in the nobler modes of life,
With sweeter manners, purer laws.

Ring out the want, the care, the sin,
The faithless coldness of the times;
Ring out, ring out my mournful rhymes,
But ring the fuller minstrel in.

狂钟敲响

阿尔弗雷德·丁尼生

狂野苍穹，狂钟敲响了，
　云朵飞驰，天光寒彻：
　岁月将于子夜中逝去；
狂钟敲响，让它死去吧！

钟声响彻，而辞旧迎新，
　欢乐钟声，回荡雪地：
　旧年将逝，让它逝去；
敲走虚假，而敲进诚挚。

敲走那侵蚀头脑之悲伤，
　因我们不再见死者；
　敲走人世穷富宿仇，
而敲进那全人类之救赎。

敲走那日渐濒危之事业、
　各方争端古旧形式；
　敲进高尚生活方式、
文雅风度而又精粹法规。

敲走贫穷、忧愁、罪愆、
　失去信仰冷酷时代；
　敲走我哀悼之韵律，
而敲进那满座吟游诗人。

Ring out false pride in place and blood,
  The civic slander and the spite;
  Ring in the love of truth and right,
Ring in the common love of good.

Ring out old shapes of foul disease,
  Ring out the narrowing lust of gold;
  Ring out the thousand wars of old,
Ring in the thousand years of peace.

Ring in the valiant man and free,
  The larger heart, the kindlier hand;
  Ring out the darkness of the land,
Ring in the Christ that is to be.

敲走名分、血统、虚荣、
　世俗人诽谤与邪恶；
　敲进真理、正义之爱，
与那些普通的慈善之爱。

敲走那疾病猖獗的陋习，
　敲走狭隘的黄金欲；
　敲走陈旧千年战争，
敲进了那和平之千禧年。

敲进英雄，以及自由权，
　心胸开阔，友善之手；
　敲走大地一片黑暗，
敲进那即将降临的基督。

Come into the Garden, Maud

Alfred Tennyson

Come into the garden, Maud,
For the black bat, Night, has flown,
Come into the garden, Maud,
I am here at the gate alone;
And the woodbine spices are wafted abroad,
And the musk of the roses blown.

For a breeze of morning moves,
And the planet of Love is on high,
Beginning to faint in the light that she loves
On a bed of daffodil sky,
To faint in the light of the sun she loves,
To faint in his light, and to die.

All night have the roses heard
The flute, violin, bassoon;
All night has the casement jessamine stirred
To the dancers dancing in tune;
Till a silence fell with the waking bird,
And a hush with the setting moon.

I said to the lily, 'There is but one
With whom she has heart to be gay.
When will the dancers leave her alone?
She is weary of dance and play.'

莫德，来这花园吧！

阿尔弗雷德·丁尼生

莫德，来这花园吧！
　因夜间黑蝙蝠已飞走。
莫德，来这花园吧！
　大门边，我独自一人。
忍冬花香气，四处飘散，
　麝香玫瑰拂动芳菲。

清晨，微风徐徐吹来，
　爱神星辰，高悬天宇；
渐渐在愉悦之晨光中，
　在乳黄天穹的卧榻上，
在愉悦之阳光下残淡，
　在光亮下衰微而逝。

玫瑰彻夜聆听：笛声、
　提琴声、巴松管乐。
窗扉上，茉莉彻夜激动，
　伴音律起舞之舞者；
直至寂静降临、鸟醒，
　静穆中，落月下沉。

我对百合说："唯一人，
　与之共享心灵欢乐。
何时舞者，离她而去？
　她厌倦跳舞与玩耍。"

Now half to the setting moon are gone.
   And half to the rising day;
Low on the sand and loud on the stone
   The last wheel echoes away.

I said to the rose, ‘The brief night goes
   In babble and revel and wine.
O young lord-lover, what sighs are those,
   For one that will never be thine?’
‘But mine, but mine,’ so I sware to the rose,
   ‘For ever and ever, mine.’

And the soul of the rose went into my blood,
   As the music clashed in the hall;
And long by the garden lake I stood,
   For I heard your rivulet fall
From the lake to the meadow and on to the wood,
   Our wood, that is dearer than all;

From the meadow your walks have left so sweet
   That whenever a March-wind sighs.
He sets the jewel-print of your feet
   In violets blue as your eyes,
To the woody hollows in which we meet
   And the valleys of Paradise.

The slender acacia would not shake
   One long milk-bloom on the tree;
The white lake-blossom fell into the lake
   As the pimpernel dozed on the lea;

此时，一半落月不见，
　另一半留于升起黎明；
沙地低音，石头高音，
　最终车轮回响离去。

我说："短暂良宵融入了
　唠叨、欢宴与美酒。
年轻恋人，叹息什么哦？
　因一人将不属于你？"
"我的，"我对之起誓：
　"永远、永远属于我。"

玫瑰灵魂流入我血液，
　音乐旋律激荡于大厅。
我久久伫立花园湖边，
　我听见：溪流从湖边、
牧场、树林而飘落下，
　此林比一切更珍弥。

每当三月风，叹息之时，
　你牧场散步洒芬芳，
珠宝般印记留于你脚下；
　明眸似蓝色紫罗兰。
葱茏山谷里，我俩相遇，
　还有天堂上的山谷。

纤细金合欢不再摇晃，
　树上盛开硕大乳白花。
雪白湖花跌落湖水里，
　牧场上，海绿草打盹。

But the rose was awake all night for your sake,
Knowing your promise to me;
The lilies and roses were all awake,
They sighed for the dawn and thee.

Queen rose of the rosebud garden of girls,
Come hither, the dances are done,
In gloss of satin and glimmer of pearls,
Queen lily and rose in one;
Shine out, little head, sunning over with curls,
To the flowers, and be their sun.

There has fallen a splendid tear
From the passion-flower at the gate.
She is coming, my dove, my dear;
She is coming, my life, my fate;
The red rose cries, 'She is near, she is near;'
And the white rose weeps, 'She is late;'
The larkspur listens, 'I hear, I hear;'
And the lily whispers, 'I wait.'

She is coming, my own, my sweet;
Were it ever so airy a tread,
My heart would hear her and beat,
Were it earth in an earthy bed;
My dust would hear her and beat,
Had I lain for a century dead;
Would start and tremble under her feet,
And blossom in purple and red.

玫瑰为你，彻夜而无眠，
　且知晓你许下诺言。
百合花与玫瑰醒来了，
　为你与黎明，长叹息。

少女花园，玫瑰花开。
　玫瑰女王来了，光彩
锦缎闪耀珍珠；舞会
　结束。百合女王与
玫瑰合一；花蕊闪烁着，
　日照卷须，百花齐放。

从大门那边，西番莲啊！
　洒落晶莹之泪珠。
她来了，亲爱的鸽子！
　啊！生命与命运。
红玫瑰喊："已走近；"
　白玫瑰哭泣："迟了；"
云雀静听："听见；"
　百合细语："等待吧。"

来了，我拥有的恋人啊！
　哪怕是轻快的脚步，
我的心听见了其声音。
　若芳土遮掩于泥床，
若我死亡，卧了一世纪，
　骨灰聆听而跳动；
在其脚下，开始战栗着，
　绽放姹紫嫣红之花。

Crossing the Bar

Alfred Tennyson

Sunset and evening star,
   And one clear call for me!
And may there be no moaning of the bar,
   When I put out to sea,

But such a tide as moving seems asleep,
   Too full for sound and foam,
When that which drew from out the boundless deep
   Turns again home.

Twilight and evening bell,
   And after that the dark!
And may there be no sadness of farewell,
   When I embark;

For tho' from out our bourne of Time and Place
   The flood may bear me far,
I hope to see my Pilot face to face
   When I have crost the bar.

穿越沙洲

阿尔弗雷德·丁尼生

落日霞飞，点点星光，
　一人清晰唤我！
或许，无沙洲在沉吟，
　当我出海而去。

潮汐起伏，酣然入眠，
　充溢喧嚣、泡沫；
它从无垠之深渊折回，
　又转回了故乡。

暮色苍茫，晚钟声声！
　在黑暗降临后，
或许，无离别之忧伤，
　当我扬帆远航。

穿越千载时空之阃限，
　潮水将游子冲远；
我希冀面晤“领航者”，
　当我穿越沙洲。

Home Thoughts, from Abroad

Robert Browning

Oh, to be in England
Now that April's there,
And whoever wakes in England
Sees, some morning, unaware,
That the lowest boughs and the brushwood sheaf
Round the elm-tree bole are in tiny leaf,
While the chaffinch sings on the orchard bough
In England— now!

And after April, when May follows,
And the whitethroat builds, and all the swallows!
Hark, where my blossomed pear-tree in the hedge
Leans to the field and scatters on the clover
Blossoms and dewdrops—at the bent spray's edge—
That's the wise thrush; he sings each song twice over,

Lest you should think he never could recapture
The first fine careless rapture!
And though the fields look rough with hoary dew.
All will be gay when noontide wakes anew
The buttercups, the little children's dower—
Far brighter than this gaudy melon-flower!

异国乡思

罗伯特・布朗宁

哦！若在英格兰，
那里，已是四月天了。
某日清晨，无论谁醒来之时，
都会不经意看见这一切：
低垂的树枝、一丛丛灌木、
榆树枝条上，缠绕鲜嫩叶子。
果园树枝上，燕雀在歌唱。
如今——在英格兰哟！

四月逝去，五月来临了。
灰莺筑巢；听吧，全然一片
燕子声！篱笆边，梨树花开，
依傍于田地。沾露之梨花，
撒满苜蓿地——弯弯喷泉边——
聪明画眉，每支歌皆唱两遍。

免得你设想：它从未被捕捉，
第一声欣喜若狂，忘乎所以！
田地因苍白露珠略呈粗糙。
一切令人愉悦：正午阳光
唤醒金凤花。孩子们之天赋——
远比俗艳之甜瓜花更靓丽啊！

Meeting at Night

Robert Browning

The gray sea and the long black land;
And the yellow half-moon large and low;
And the startled little waves that leap
In fiery ringlets from their sleep,
As I gain the cove with pushing prow,
And quench its speed i' the slushy sand.

Then a mile of warm sea-scented beach;
Three fields to cross till a farm appears;
A tap at the pane, the quick sharp scratch
And blue spurt of a lighted match,
And a voice less loud, thro' its joys and fears
Than the two hearts beating each to each!

夜间幽会

罗伯特·勃朗宁

灰色大海、广袤黑土之上：
金色半月，硕大而又低悬。
微波从安眠中，而被惊醒，
在湍急漩涡之中，跃动着。
我划动小舟，接近小海湾，
在泥泞之沙地，停止行驶。

一英里海滩弥漫温馨腥味；
我穿越三块田，农庄隐现。
我轻敲窗棂，迅疾划火柴，
它迸发一团蓝色小火焰。
两颗相拥之心，怦怦直跳，
远响亮于又惊又喜的细语。

The Last Ride Together（Excerpt）

Robert Browning

I

I said—then, dearest, since 'tis so,
Since now at length my fate I know,
Since nothing all my love avails,
Since all, my life seemed meant for, fails,
Since this was written and needs must be—
My whole heart rises up to bless
Your name in pride and thankfulness!
Take back the hope you gave, —I claim
—Only a memory of the same,
—And this beside, if you will not blame,
Your leave for one more last ride with me.

最后一起骑马（节选）

罗伯特·勃朗宁

I

我说——亲爱的，既然如此；
既然我最终晓得：自身命运，
既然没什么有利于我的爱情，
既然我生命，似乎意味失去，
既然一切已记录，必然需要——
我整个心灵飞跃起而去祝福：
你的名字，多么自豪而感恩！
收回你赐予的希望，我申明：
——仅这次同样美好的记忆；
此外，假若你将来不受责怪，
就再次留下最后骑马的回忆。

A Little While, a Little While

Emily Bronte

A little while, a little while
The noisy crowd, are barred away;
And I can sing and I can smile
A little while I have holiday!

Where wilt thou go my harassed heart?
Full many a land invites thee now;
And places near, and far apart
Have rest for thee, my weary brow—

There is a spot 'mid barren hills
Where winter howls, and driving rain
But if the dreary tempest chills
There is a light that warms again

The house is old, the trees are bare
And moonless above bends the misty dome
But what on earth is half so dear—
So longed for as the hearth of home?

The mute bird sitting on the stone,
The dank moss dripping from the wall,
The garden-walk with weeds.
I love them— how I love them all!

一小会儿，一小会儿

艾米莉·勃朗特

一小会儿，一小会儿，
嘈杂人群挡在外面；
我能唱歌，我能欢笑，
我欢度假日一小会儿！

我烦恼之心将去哪里？
整个茫茫大地邀请；
远远近近，各处隔开，
让我疲倦的额头休憩——

在荒凉山陵里有一处：
冬季，狂风暴雨呼啸；
若阴冷之风颇有寒意，
还有光亮，给予温馨。

古旧房宅，光秃树林，
迷蒙蒙天穹却无月光；
究竟什么几近于珍弥——
那么渴求于家庭炉火？

喑哑鸟雀，栖于岩石，
阴湿苔藓墙上在滴水；
花园小径，野草疯长，
我喜欢、深爱这一切！

Shall I go there? or shall I seek
Another clime, another sky.
Where tongues familiar music speak
In accents dear to memory?

Yes, as I mused, the naked room,
The flickering firelight died away
And from the midst of cheerless gloom
I passed to bright, unclouded day—

A little and a lone green lane
That opened on a common wide,
A distant, dreamy, dim blue chain
Of mountains circling every side—

A heaven so clear, an earth so calm,
So sweet, so soft, so hushed an air;
And, deepening still the dream-like charm,
Wild moor-sheep feeding everywhere—

That was the scene, I knew it well
I knew the pathways far and near
That winding o'er each billowy swell
Marked out the tracks of wandering deer.

Could I have lingered but an hour
It well had paid a week of toil
But truth has banished fancy's power
I hear my dungeon bars recoil—

我将去哪？我将寻觅
另一风土，另一苍穹。
那熟悉音乐之方言，
对于记忆，尤为珍贵。

我沉思着，空荡房间，
摇曳的火光已熄灭了；
在阴郁不快的氛围中，
我来到一片万里晴空。

一条孤寂的绿色小巷，
它以一般宽度而敞开；
青色山峦环绕着四周，
遥远、梦幻，又模糊——

天那么清，地那么静，
空气甜润，柔和肃穆，
愈发加深梦幻之魅力；
旷野，处处羊群吃草。

这也是我熟知的景观：
那些远远近近的小径，
盘绕着波涛一般山丘；
标记着小鹿儿的游踪。

若我流连一小时光景，
就需付出一周的辛苦；
真相驱逐幻想之魔力，
我听见自己打开牢栅——

Even as I stood with raptured eye
Absorbed in bliss so deep and dear
My hour of rest had fleeted by
And given me back to weary care—

我以欣喜眼神伫立着，
深深地沉浸难得福祉；
我生命之余光在飞逝，
又返回那疲倦、忧虑——

Sudden Light

Dante Rossetti

I have been here before,
　But when or how I cannot tell:
I know the grass beyond the door,
　The sweet keen smell,
The sighing sound, the lights around the shore.

You have been mine before,—
　How long ago I may not know:
But just when at that swallow's soar
　Your neck turned so,
Some veil did fall, — I knew it all of yore.

Has this been thus before?
　And shall not thus time's eddying flight
Still with our lives our love restore
　In death's despite,
And day and night yield one delight once more?

蓦然之光

但丁·罗塞蒂

往昔，我也曾经在此处，
　何时？如何？不可告知：
我晓得，门口那边草地上，
　散发一阵阵浓烈香味；
叹息声、灯光弥漫着那海滨。

往昔，你也曾经属于我——
　很久前，或许我不知晓：
正值燕子呢喃翻飞之际，
　你扭颈朝上仰望着，
面纱果真落下，我知晓往昔。

往昔一切，也曾经如此吗？
　如此时光，不会再飞旋；
在死亡威胁之下，生活、
　爱情将仍会欣欣然复苏，
昼夜将会再次产生一种欢乐？

Up-Hill

Christina Rossetti

Does the road wind up-hill all the way?
Yes, to the very end.
Will the day's journey take the whole long day?
From morn to night, my friend.

But is there for the night a resting-place?
A roof for when the slow dark hours begin.
May not the darkness hide it from my face?
You cannot miss that inn.

Shall I meet other wayfarers at night?
Those who have gone before.
Then must I knock, or call when just in sight?
They will not keep you standing at that door.

Shall I find comfort, travel-sore and weak?
Of labour you shall find the sum.
Will there be beds for me and all who seek?
Yea, beds for all who come.

上 山

克里丝蒂娜·罗塞蒂

路上狂风一直刮至山顶？
　是的，刮至最端头。
白昼旅行要花费一整天？
　从早至晚，朋友。

夜间可有一个歇脚之处？
　顶屋专为日暮之用。
黑暗不会从我脸上隐去？
　你不能错过客栈。

夜间我会遇见其他游客？
　他人早已走了。
我必须敲门或见人就召唤？
　不会让你久留于门外。

旅途又苦又累，有舒适处？
　劳顿总付出代价。
我与寄宿者可有床铺吗？
　是的，为来客已备好。

Summer Dawn

William Morris

Pray but one prayer for me 'twixt thy closed lips,
Think but one thought of me up in the stars.
  The summer night waneth, the morning light slips,
Faint and grey 'twixt the leaves of the aspen, betwixt the cloud-bars,
That are patiently waiting there for the dawn:
  Patient and colourless, though Heaven's gold
Waits to float through them along with the sun.
Far out in the meadows, above the young corn,
  The heavy elms wait, and restless and cold
The uneasy wind rises; the roses are dun;
Through the long twilight they pray for the dawn.
Round the lone house in the midst of the corn.
  Speak but one word to me over the corn,
  Over the tender, bow'd locks of the corn.

夏日黎明

威廉·莫里斯

你启唇仅为我作此祷文而祈祷，
我仅以此想象之想象直冲星际。
夏夜消融，晨光残淡而灰白，
渗入杨树叶间；在云朵光栅间。
那里一切耐心地期待黎明来临：
耐心而苍白；天穹上金光灿灿，
与太阳光期待着：飘浮于大地。
远至牧场里，或小谷苗之上，
沉郁榆树在等待，骚动而冷淡。
风儿不安而刮起，玫瑰颇阴郁；
在漫漫熹微中，皆为黎明祈祷。
在谷地之间，在孤寂房宅四周，
你对我说的片语飘拂于谷苗上，
飘拂于一束束温柔的弯弯谷物。

When I Set Out for Lyonnesse

Thomas Hardy

When I set out for Lyonnesse,
A hundred miles away,
The rime was on the spray,
And starlight lit my lonesomeness
When I set out for Lyonnesse
A hundred miles away.

What would bechance at Lyonnesse
While I should sojourn there
No prophet durst declare,
Nor did the wisest wizard guess
What would bechance at Lyonnesse
While I should sojourn there.

When I came back from Lyonnesse
With magic in my eyes,
All marked with mute surmise.
My radiance rare and fathomless,
When I came back from Lyonnesse
With magic in my eyes!

我出发去利昂纳赛

托马斯·哈代

我出发去利昂纳赛，
　一百英里之遥，
　听着浪花节奏；
星光照耀孤寂之心，
我出发去利昂纳赛，
　一百英里之遥。

利昂纳赛有何机缘？
　我旅居在那里，
　无先知挑战声言，
也无神通术士预测。
利昂纳赛有何机缘？
　我旅居在那里。

我从利昂纳赛返回，
　目光充溢魔力，
　默揣所有标识。
我从利昂纳赛返回，
目光充溢了魔力，
　发珍奇深邃之光！

Snow in the Suburbs

Thomas Hardy

Every branch big with it,
Bent every twig with it;
Every fork like a white web-foot;
Every street and pavement mute:
Some flakes have lost their way, and grope back
upward, when
Meeting those meandering down they turn and
descend again.
The palings are glued together like a wall,
And there is no waft of wind with the fleecy fall.

A sparrow enters the tree,
Whereon immediately
A snow-lump thrice his own slight size
Descends on him and showers his head and eyes.
And overturns him,
And near inurns him,
And lights on a nether twig, when its brush
Starts off a volley of other lodging lumps with a rush.

The steps are a blanched slope,
Up which, with feeble hope,
A black cat comes, wide-eyed and thin;
And we take him in.

郊区的雪

托马斯·哈代

每一树干覆盖着厚雪，
白雪将每根细枝压弯了；
每一树杈似白色鸟蹼之印记。
每条街衢、人行道，一片喑哑：
纷纷雪花迷失了，摸摸索索着，
返回了天空。当飘舞雪片时，
碰见曲曲折折之路，遂又转回去；
再洒落下来。
条条篱笆紧紧胶着，似一堵墙，
无风飘拂那洒落羊绒似的白雪。

一只麻雀飞进树丛里，
在那里，一刹那时，
大片雪块有它体积三倍大，
降临于它，似阵雨一般浇淋于
它头上和眼窝。它倾覆于一旦，
几乎似瓮罐罩住。
它轻歇于细枝；掠过时，
却冲起一阵堆砌雪块的骤然喷发哟。

台阶变成了雪白色斜坡。
其上方，黑猫来了，
怀着渺茫希望，睁圆眼而羸弱；
我们收留了它。

The Oxen

Thomas Hardy

Christmas Eve, and twelve of the clock.
　　'Now they are all on their knees,'
An elder said as we sat in a flock
　By the embers in hearthside ease.

We pictured the meek mild creatures where
　They dwelt in their strawy pen,
Nor did it occur to one of us there
　To doubt they were kneeling then.

So fair a fancy few would weave
　In these years! Yet, I feel,
If someone said on Christmas Eve,
　　'Come; see the oxen kneel

In the lonely barton by yonder coomb
　Our childhood used to know,'
I should go with him in the gloom,
　Hoping it might be so.

公　牛

托马斯·哈代

圣诞前夕，钟声十二响：
　“此时它们全跪下；”
长者说：我们成群闲坐，
　在尚有余烬的炉边。

我们想象：温顺而善良
　牲畜，栖于麦秸圈。
而其中，谁都不会对此
　怀疑：公牛正跪着。

这年头，如此美妙幻景，
　很少人编织！我想：
若圣诞节前夕，有人说：
　“来！瞧公牛跪在

那边峡谷一个寂静农场；
　我们童年经常知晓。”
我应与他一起去昏暗处，
　祈求着如愿以偿。

Channel Firing

Thomas Hardy

That night your great guns, unawares,
Shook all our coffins as we lay,
And broke the chancel window-squares,
We thought it was the judgment-day.

And sat up straight. While drearisome
Arose the howl of weakened hounds:
The mouse let fall the altar-crumb,
The worms drew back into the mounds,

The glebe cow drooled. Till God called, "No;
It's gunnery practice out at sea
Just as before you went below;
The world is as it used to be:

"All nations striving strong to make
Red war yet redder. Mad as hatters
They do no more for Christ's sake
Than you who are helpless in such matters

"That this is not the judgment-hour
For some of them's a blessed thing,
For if it were they'd have to scour
Hell's floor for so much threatening...

海峡的炮火

托马斯·哈代

那夜间，你们火炮突然地：
震动所有我们卧着的棺材。
教堂里，圣坛和窗框断裂；
我们认为这是一个审判日。

我们笔直坐起，传来一阵
惊醒猎犬嚎叫，毛骨悚然。
耗子却使圣坛上碎屑落下；
蛆虫畏缩着，又钻入土堆。

草地上母牛流涎。上帝说：
“不”，炮兵在大海边演习，
正如你们到来阴间之前；
这世界上，仍是一如既往：

所有国家努力强国，将使
赤红战争更赤红。以基督
名义，发狂的他们不再做；
无助的你们，也不做此事。

对于一些颇有福气的人们，
这也并非审判之时刻。
若他们为了这么多的威胁，
就必须去冲刷地狱的地板……

"Ha, ha. It will be warmer when
I below the trumpet (if indeed
I even do; for you are men,
And rest eternal sorely need). "

So down we lay again. "I wonder,
Will the world ever saner be,"
Said one, "than when He sent us under
In our indifferent century!"

And many a skeleton shook his head.
"Instead of preaching forty years,"
My neighbor Parson Thirdly said,
"I wish I had stuck to pipes and beer."

Again the guns disturbed the hour,
Roaring their readiness to avenge ,
As far inland as Stourton Tower,
And Camelot, and starlit Stonehenge.

“哈哈！当我吹响了号角时，
它将会变得更热烈。(若我
确实曾做过，因你们男人，
也极为需要一种永久休息。）”

故我们又卧下。一个人说：
“真奇怪：这世界比上帝送——
我们去阴间时更明智吧!
在我们这冷漠无情的世纪!”

许多骷髅全都摇晃着脑袋。
我的邻人帕森，第三个说：
“我希望迷恋烟斗、啤酒，
而不是去祈祷了40年之久。”

轰隆炮火声，又打扰时光，
怒吼着：其迅疾的复仇；
远至那内陆的斯图顿之塔、
卡莫洛特、星光辉耀巨石阵。

Hurrahing in Harvest

Gerard Hopkins

Summer ends now; now, barbarous in beauty, the stooks rise
   Around; up above, what wind-walks! what lovely behaviour
   Of silk-sack clouds! has wilder, wilful-wavier
Meal-drift moulded ever and melted across skies?

I walk, I lift up, I lift up heart, eyes,
   Down all that glory in the heavens to glean our Saviour:
   And, eyes, heart, what looks, what lips yet gave you a
Rapturous love's greeting of realer, of rounder replies?

And the azurous hung hills are his world-wielding shoulder
   Majestic—as a stallion stalwart, very-violet-sweet—
These things, these things were here and but the beholder

   Wanting; which two when they once meet,
The heart rears wings bold and bolder
   And hurls for him, O half hurls earth for him off under his feet.

收获节的欢呼声

吉拉德·霍普金斯

此时夏天结束，粗野之美，禾束堆从周遭
　飞起；飞至天穹，多么行走如风！多可爱
　丝带云彩飘动！是否曾有更狂野的任意
挥舞、粗粉飞扬的沃土在溶解并穿越天穹？

我行走，又飘起；我神采飞扬，而又举目
　朝下，天堂一切荣耀寻觅我们救世主。
　而眼睛、心脏、何种目光、唇吻，给你
狂喜爱情的问候更真实，而又圆满的答复？

碧空高悬山陵，它庄严地焊接世界的肩头，
　——犹高大而健壮的雄马、紫罗兰芳香！——
这些事嘛，这些事都在此显现，而观看者

　所匮乏的。当他俩曾经相遇的时候，
心脏掀起了翼动，大胆愈发大胆。
　掷向他，哦！半掷的泥土使之双脚腾起。

The Windhover

Gerard Hopkins

I caught this morning morning's minion, kingdom
  of daylight's dauphin, dapple-dawn-drawn Falcon, in his riding
  Of the rolling level underneath him steady air, and striding
High there, how he rung upon the rein of a wimpling wing
In his ecstasy! then off, off forth on swing,
  As a skate's heel sweeps smooth on a bow-bend : the hurl and gliding
  Rebuffed the big wind. My heart in hiding
Stirred for a bird,—the achieve of, the mastery of the thing!

Brute beauty and valour and act, oh, air, pride, plume, here
  Buckle! and the fire that breaks from thee then, a billion
Times told lovelier, more dangerous. O my chevalier!

  No wonder of it: shéer plód makes plough down sillion
Shine, and blue-bleak embers, ah my dear,
  Fall, gall themselves, and gash gold-vermilion.

茶　隼

吉拉德·霍普金斯

清晨，我仰望着晨曦的庞幸儿，
　黎明王国之太子，斑斓晨光之游隼，
　在滚滚云层上翱翔，下方湍湍气流；
它高高盘旋，展开弯曲飞翼，啼鸣着，
多么狂喜！飞啊飞，自由地前往，
　似滑冰鞋平滑地掠过彩虹；时而猛冲，
　时而滑翔，挫败飓风。我深沉之心，
为飞鸟成功、精湛之技能——而鼓舞！

粗野之美、刚毅、敏捷，啊！高傲、
　气流、羽毛在此变形！内在迸发火焰，
无数次告诫：越美越危险。啊！骑士！

　难怪乎：仅辛劳耕耘，土地才能收获。
灰黑余烬也会闪耀光焰，啊！亲爱的，
　摔打、磨炼，伤口流金色而朱红之血。

Renouncement

Alice Meynell

I must not think of thee; and, tired yet strong,
I shun the love that lurks in all delight—
The love of thee—and in the blue Heaven's height,
And in the sweetest passage of a song.

Oh, just beyond the fairest thoughts that throng
This breast, the thought of thee waits, hidden yet bright;
But it must never, never come in sight;
I must stop short of thee the whole day long.

But when sleep comes to close each diffcult day,
When night gives pause to the long watch I keep,
And all my bonds I need must loose apart,

Must doff my will as raiment laid away,—
With the first dream that comes with the first sleep
I run, I run, I am gathered to thy heart.

抛　弃

艾丽丝·梅纳尔

我不必思念；疲惫而坚持，
　避开潜伏于喜悦之情思——
对你的爱——在蔚蓝高空上，
在最甜美的歌曲乐章里。

哦！最美之情愫孕育于胸怀，
　期待着，隐匿而又明亮。
　而它永不，永不展现眼前；
我必整天警惕，突然阻止你。

睡眠来临于每一艰难的白昼，
　黑夜暂停了我那久久警戒。
　　我所需一切束缚必松懈。

我必抛弃意志，如脱去衣饰——
　在梦乡初启之刻酣然入睡。
　　我跑啊跑，聚拢你心房。

The Lamplighter

Robert Stevenson

My tea is nearly ready and the sun has left the sky;
It's time to take the window to see Leerie going by;
For every night at teatime and before you take your seat,
With lantern and with ladder he comes posting up the street.

Now Tom would be a driver and Maria go to sea,
And my papa's a banker and as rich as he can be;
But I, when I am stronger and can choose what I'm to do,
O Leerie, I'll go round at night and light the lamps with you!

For we are very lucky, with a lamp before the door,
And Leerie stops to light it as he lights so many more;
And O! before you hurry by with ladder and with light,
O Leerie, see a little child and nod to him to-night!

点灯的人

罗伯特·斯蒂文森

我的茶快要准备好，太阳已西沉了，
推开窗户可以瞧见利里在此经过。
每天傍晚饮茶时分，在你就座之前，
他手拿着提灯，并登梯挂在大街上。

此时，汤姆是司机，玛利亚去海边。
我爸爸是一位银行家，足够富有。
当我长大强壮，就能选择一种行当。
哦！利里和我夜晚点灯，四处转悠！

我们真幸运！大门前有了一盏明灯，
利里点燃着许多灯，终于停止点灯。
哦！利里，在你匆忙登梯燃亮灯前，
哦！若见小孩点头致意，道声晚安！

Tell Me Not Here

Afred Housman

Tell me not here, it needs not saying,
What tune the enchantress plays
In aftermaths of soft September
Or under blanching mays,
For she and I were long acquainted
And I knew all her ways.

On russet floors, by waters idle,
The pine lets fall its cone;
The cuckoo shouts all day at nothing
In leafy dells alone;
And traveller's joy beguiles in autumn
Hearts that have lost their own.

On acres of the seeded grasses
The changing burnish heaves;
Or marshalled under moons of harvest
Stand still all night the sheaves;
Or beeches strip in storms for winter
And stain the wind with leaves.

Possess, as I possessed a season,
The countries I resign,
Where over elmy plains the highway
Would mount the hills and shine,

说我不在此

阿尔弗雷德·豪斯曼

说我不在此，也不必要说，
　女巫演奏什么曲调？
在温和九月天的尾声之际，
　在遮阳的山楂树下，
因为我与她曾经多年相识，
　我了解她的一切。

赤褐地板上，悠悠流水中，
　松树坠落下松果；
在枝叶茂密山谷里，杜鹃
　整日乏味地独自啁啾。
秋季，游子们寻欢、消遣，
　心里却是失去自我。

在那数亩长种籽的草地上，
　光亮起伏而又变幻；
月光下，一束束收获庄稼，
　排列成行，彻夜静立。
冬季狂风中，山毛榉剥落，
　风轻轻染色于树叶。

拥有，犹如拥有一个季节，
　我辞别了小乡村；
那里平原长满榆树。公路
　攀缘丘陵上，闪耀着；

And full of shade the pillared forest
   Would murmur and be mine.

For nature, heartless, witless nature,
   Will neither care nor know
What stranger's feet may find the meadow
   And trespass there and go,
Nor ask amid the dews of morning
   If they are mine or no.

林立之森林，却充满荫影，
　总是絮语，而属于我。

大自然，毫无情商与智性，
　既不在乎，也不知道：
陌生人脚步已发现草场，
　侵入那里，又走开。
在清晨露珠中，勿要询问：
　它们是否也属于我。

Loveliest of Trees, the Cherry Now

Afred Housman

Loveliest of trees, the cherry now
Is hung with bloom along the bough,
And stands about the woodland ride
Wearing white for Eastertide.

Now, of my threescore years and ten,
Twenty will not come again,
And take from seventy springs a score,
It only leaves me fifty more.

And since to look at things in bloom
Fifty springs are little room,
About the woodlands I will go
To see the cherry hung with snow.

最可爱的树，此时樱桃花

阿尔弗雷德·豪斯曼

最可爱的树，樱桃花
绽放，挂满树枝上；
花树林立，白衣使者，
驰传复活节之讯息。

知天命之年再加十岁，
二十年光阴已不复返；
七十春减去飞逝岁月，
唯留于我五十余年。

自从观赏樱桃树开花，
半世纪之春一瞬间；
我环绕着林地而漫步，
欣赏玉树儿挂满雪花。

1887

Alfred Housman

From Clee to heaven the beacon burns,
The shires have seen it plain,
From north and south the sign returns
and beacons burn again.

Look left, look right, the hills are bright,
The dales are light between,
Because 'tis fifty years tonight
That God has saved the Queen.

Now, when the flame they watch not towers
About the soil they trod,
Lads, we'll remember friends of ours
Who shared the work with God.

To skies that knit their heartstrings right,
To fields that bred them brave,
The saviors come not home tonight:
Themselves they could not save.

It dawns in Asia, tombstones show
And Shropshire names are read;
And the Nile spills his overflow
Beside the Severn's dead.

1887年

阿尔弗雷德·豪斯曼

克利山灯塔，照亮天穹，
　中部郡皆清晰可见；
从南至北，信号返回时，
　火炬又熊熊燃烧起。

环顾四周，群山皆通亮，
　其溪谷间，光影闪烁。
今夜50周年庆典！国歌
　响起：上帝拯救女王。

如今，他们所见的光焰，
　不再普照曾踏过土地；
士兵，我们铭记的朋友——
　却在分担上帝的事业。

蔚蓝天穹，打动其心弦，
　战场上，培育其勇气。
今夜，救世军不再回国：
　却再不能拯救了自己。

亚洲黎明时分，墓碑上，
　显现希罗郡士兵名字。
在塞文河畔的死难者旁，
　泛滥尼罗河水淹没他。

We pledge in peace by farm and town
  The Queen they served in war,
And fire the beacons up and down
  The land they perished for.

"God save the Queen"[1] we living sing,
  From height to height 'tis heard;
And with the rest your voices ring,
  Lads of the Fifty- third.

Oh, God will save her, fear you not:
  Be you're the men you've been,
Get you the sons your fathers got,
  And God will save the Queen.

注：①"God save the Queen"是英国国歌的歌词，在庆典会仪式上经常咏唱。诗人豪斯曼以讽喻而又批判的语气，揭露了大英帝国的昔日繁荣都是普通士兵用生命换来的。

在乡镇，我们静静宣誓；
　战争中军队效忠女王。
火炬光焰，正上下摆动，
　士兵在这片土地捐躯。

活者唱：“上帝拯救女王”，
　歌声越过一座座高地；
53步兵团士兵歌声响起，
　伴随其他人正在合唱。

上帝拯救女王，莫怕哟！
　做你们曾是的男子汉；
让子子孙孙像父辈后代，
　上帝将会拯救女王。

With Rues My Heart Is Laden

Edward Housman

With rue my heart is laden
For golden friends I had,
For marry a rose-lipt maiden
And many a lightfoot lad.

By brooks too broad for leaping
The lightfoot boys are laid;
The rose-lipt girls are sleeping
In fields where roses fade.

我的心充满了忧伤

爱德华·豪斯曼

我的心儿，充满忧伤：
为我拥有的金兰之交，
为唇红如玫瑰之少女，
和那健步如飞的少年。

那健步如飞的少年，
安卧无从飞跃的溪边；
唇红如玫瑰之少女，
沉睡花儿凋谢的田间。

Down by the Salley Gardens

William Yeats

Down by the salley gardens my love and I did meet;
She passed the salley gardens with little snow-white feet.
She bid me take love easy, as the leaves grow on the tree;
But I, being young and foolish, with her would not agree.

In a field by the river my love and I did stand,
And on my leaning shoulder she laid her snow-white hand.
She bid me take life easy, as the grass grows on the weirs;
But I was young and foolish, and now am full of tears.

沿着萨利花园

威廉·叶芝

我的恋人沿着萨利花园，我迎她；
她踏着雪白小脚，穿行美丽花园。
她叮嘱从容爱着，犹绿叶长树上；
而我年轻、傻气与之想法不一样。

我的恋人在河边田野里，我站着；
她以雪白纤手，抚摸我瘦弱肩头。
她叮嘱从容生活，犹青草长堰上；
而我年轻、傻气，此时泪流满面。

The Song of Wandering Aengus

William Yeats

I went out to the hazel wood,
Because a fire was in my head,
And cut and peeled a hazel wand,
And hooked a berry to a thread;
And when white moths were on the wing,
And moth-like stars were flickering out,
I dropped the berry in a stream
And caught a little silver trout.

When I had laid it on the floor,
I went to blow the fire aflame,
But something rustled on the floor,
And some one called me by my name:
It had become a glimmering girl
With apple blossom in her hair
Who called me by my name and ran
And faded through the brightening air.

Though I am old with wandering
Through hollow lands and hilly lands,
I will find out where she has gone,
And kiss her lips and take her hands;
And walk among long dappled grass,
And pluck till time and times are done
The silver apples of the moon,
The golden apples of the sun.

漫游安格斯之歌

威廉·叶芝

我去红褐色榛树林，
因心中一团火焰；
切开并剥下榛树枝，
勾住浆果悬挂绳上。
白蛾正拍翅飞舞时，
似那星辰闪烁再现；
我把浆果扔在小溪，
捉一条银色小鳟鱼。

我将之置于地板上，
且去打造通红炉火。
地面上某物沙沙响，
有人在呼唤我名字；
变为闪微光的少女，
发束上簪着苹果花。
她刚称呼我就跑走，
从发亮气流中残淡。

我暮年时四处漫游，
穿越低凹处与丘陵；
我将何处去寻觅她？
而与之亲吻并牵手；
漫步于斑驳草地时，
采撷明月上银苹果，
采撷红日上金苹果，
直至时光地老天荒。

The Fiddler of Dooney

William Yeats

When I play on my fiddle in Dooney,
Folk dance like a wave of the sea;
My cousin is priest in Kilvarnet,
My brother in Mocharabuiee.

I passed my brother and cousin:
They read in their books of prayer;
I read in my book of songs;
I bought at the Sligo fair.

When we come at the end of time
To Peter sitting in state,
He will smile on the three old spirits,
But call me first through the gate;

For the good are always the merry,
Save by an evil chance,
And the merry love the fiddle,
And the merry love to dance:

And when the folk there spy me,
They will all come up to me,
With 'Here is the fiddler of Dooney!'
And dance like a wave of the sea.

多莱的提琴师

威廉·叶芝

我在多莱拉提琴时,
乡亲跳舞好似海浪;
表兄是基瓦莱牧师,
兄弟住在莫哈拉布。

我拜访兄弟与表兄,
他俩正读着祈祷书;
歌本从斯莱戈市场
买来,我也正阅读。

结束时,我们来到
庄重就座彼得面前;
他对三老笑容可掬,
并召唤我先出大门。

善良人总是乐天派,
从恶运之中而获救;
提琴弹奏欢乐之爱,
舞蹈跳起欢乐之爱。

那里乡亲见到我时,
纷纷走到我面前说:
“多莱的提琴师!”
而舞蹈似大海波浪。

The Way through the Woods

Rudyard Kipling

They shut the road through the woods
Seventy years ago.
Weather and rain have undone it again,
And now you would never know
There was once a road through the woods
Before they planted the trees.
It is underneath the coppice and heath
And the thin anemones.
Only the keeper sees
That, where the ring-dove broods,
And the badgers roll at ease,
There was once a road through the woods.

Yet, if you enter the woods
Of a summer evening late,
When the night-air cools on the trout-ringed pools
Where the otter whistles his mate,
(They fear not men in the woods,
Because they see so few)
You will hear the beat of a horse's feet,
And the swish of a skirt in the dew,
Steadily cantering through
The misty solitudes,
As though they perfectly knew
The old lost road through the woods...
But there is no road through the woods.

那穿越树林之路

鲁迪亚·吉卜林

七十年前，他们封闭了
穿越树林之路；
天气与雨水将之又毁坏。
此时，你从不知道：
那曾经有穿越树林之路，
在他们植树之前。
它在灌木丛，荒野里与
那些稀疏的海葵之下方。
只有守林者才能望见；
还有铃鸽，正在孵窝，
灰獾悠闲地滚滚而动；
那曾经有穿越树林之路。

夏日夜幕，降临了树林；
倘若你走进它，
鳟鱼环池上，夜气凉爽；
水獭尖啸，呼唤配偶。
（它们不怕林中有他人，
因其视力几近茫然。）
你会听见一阵阵马蹄声，
和露水中衣裙的窸窣声。
马儿平稳溜达，穿越了
迷雾缥缈之孤寂。
虽然他们往昔极其熟悉：
那穿越树林迷失之老路……
现在却无穿越树林之路。

If–

Rudyard Kipling

If you can keep your head when all about you
　Are losing theirs and blaming it on you,
If you can trust yourself when all men doubt you,
　But make allowance for their doubting too;
If you can wait and not be tired by waiting,
　Or being lied about, don't deal in lies,
Or being hated, don't give way to hating,
　And yet don't look too good, nor talk too wise:

If you can dream—and not make dreams your master;
　If you can think—and not make thoughts your aim:
If you can meet with Triumph and Disaster
　And treat those two impostors just the same;
If you can bear to hear the truth you've spoken
　Twisted by knaves to make a trap for fools,
Or watch the things you gave your life to, broken,
　And stoop and build 'em up with worn-out tools.

If you can make one heap of all your winnings
　And risk it on one turn of pitch-and-toss,
And lose, and start again at your beginnings
　And never breathe a word about your loss;
If you can force your heart and nerve and sinew
　To serve your turn long after they are gone,
And so hold on when there is nothing in you

假如——

鲁迪亚·吉卜林

若你保持清醒，而周围人，
　正失去理智，并责怪于你。
若你自信，所有人怀疑你；
　你对之怀疑，却以示辩解。
若你能等待，勿因此厌烦；
　四周是撒谎，勿因此谎言。
若有仇恨，勿因此而抱怨；
　不要太乐观，不自作聪明。

若做梦——不让梦幻主宰；
　若你思考——欲速则不达。
若你碰见胜利与灾难之时，
　仅当作同样对付两个骗子。
若你能忍受你曾说的真相，
　恶棍歪曲，为傻子设陷阱；
或你用生命呵护之物遭破坏，
　屈从以磨损工具将之修补。

若你赢得一大堆的成功之后，
　在巅峰下跌的险关中冒险。
你失败之后，又重新开始，
　从不说一句灰心丧气的话。
若你迫使那衰竭心脏、神经、
　肌腱再重新振作，而适用。
当你空空如也，那么坚持吧！

　Except the Will which says to them: ‘Hold on!’

If you can talk with crowds and keep your virtue,
　Or walk with Kings—nor lose the common touch,
If neither foes nor loving friends can hurt you,
　If all men count with you, but none too much;
If you can fill the unforgiving minute
　With sixty seconds’ worth of distance run,
Yours is the Earth and everything that’s in it,
　And—which is more—you’ll be a Man, my son!

　　除了意志对之说："坚持！"

若你与群众说话，保持美德；
　　与国王行走，不失去联系。
若仇敌与好友，不能伤害你；
　　大家取宠你，却也不过分。
若你能花费60秒钟短程跑，
　　填满了无情飞逝的一分钟——
你拥有地球，它包罗万象。
尤为重要：孩子，做个汉子！

I Have Been Faithful to Thee

Ernest Dowson

Last night, ah, yesternight, betwixt her lips and mine
There fell thy shadow, Cynara! thy breath was shed
Upon my soul between the kisses and the wine;
And I was desolate and sick of an old passion,
   Yea, I was desolate and bowed my head:
I have been faithful to thee, Cynara! in my fashion.

All night upon mine heart I felt her warm heart beat,
Night-long within mine arms in love and sleep she lay;
Surely the kisses of her bought red mouth were sweet;
But I was desolate and sick of an old passion,
   When I awoke and found the dawn was gray:
I have been faithful to thee, Cynara! in my fashion.

I have forgot much, Cynara! gone with the wind,
Flung roses, roses riotously with the throng,
Dancing, to put thy pale, lost lilies out of mind;
But I was desolate and sick of an old passion,
   Yea, all the time, because the dance was long:
I have been faithful to thee, Cynara! in my fashion.

I cried for madder music and for stronger wine,
But when the feast is finished and the lamps expire,
Then falls thy shadow, Cynara! the night is thine;
And I am desolate and sick of an old passion,
   Yea hungry for the lips of my desire:
I have been faithful to thee, Cynara! in my fashion.

我忠诚于你

欧内斯特·道森

昨夜啊！昨夜她与我唇边落下：
你的阴影。赛纳拉！你的呼吸
流淌于我灵魂，亲吻与美酒间；
我孤独而凄凉，思念往日激情。
　是的，我孤苦而低垂下头：
赛纳拉！以我的方式忠诚于你。

整夜，她温暖之心与我齐跳动，
沉浸在爱情中，依偎我的怀抱；
无疑，她的红唇之吻如此甜蜜，
我孤独而凄凉，思念往日激情。
　当我醒来，却发现灰色黎明：
赛纳拉！以我的方式忠诚于你。

赛纳拉！忘怀颇多，随风飘去，
与人群纵情地掷去玫瑰、玫瑰。
跳舞吧！将残淡百合抛至脑后；
我孤独而凄凉，思念往日激情。
　是的，始终久久地翩翩起舞：
赛纳拉！以我的方式忠诚于你。

我呼唤：狂放旋律、浓烈美酒！
宴会结束，灯光熄灭时，落下
你阴影。赛纳拉！今宵属于你。
我孤独而凄凉，思念往日激情。
　是的，渴求我欲望之唇吻：
赛纳拉！以我的方式忠诚于你。

The Little Dancers

Robert Binyon

Lonely, save for a few faint stars, the sky
Dreams; and lonely, below, the little street
Into its gloom retires, secluded and shy.
Scarcely the dumb roar enters this soft retreat;
And all is dark, save where come flooding rays
From a tavern-window; there, to the brisk measure
Of an organ that down in an alley merrily plays,
Two children, all alone and no one by,
Holding their tattered frocks, thro' an airy maze
Of motion lightly threaded with nimble feet
Dance sedately; face to face they gaze,
Their eyes shining, grave with a perfect pleasure.

小舞者

罗伯特 · 宾昂

寂寥啊！除了几颗暗淡星辰，
苍天梦幻；下方小街孤寂，
在幽暗中隐退，封闭而羞涩。
罕见喑哑的吼声进入幽静处；
一切皆黑暗，除了酒馆窗户
透出泛光灯。在底下小巷里，
风琴快乐地演奏轻松之旋律。
两个孩子很孤苦，无人过往；
他们握着褴褛外衣，灵巧而
轻踩舞步，穿越气流之迷津。
祥和舞蹈；彼此面对面凝视，
炯炯闪光眼睛，庄严而喜悦。

The Farmer's Bride

Charlotte Mew

Three Summers since I chose a maid,
Too young maybe— but more's to do
At harvest-time than bide and woo.
  When us was wed she turned afraid
Of love and me and all things human;
Like the shut of a winter's day.
Her smile went out, and 'twasn't a woman—
  More like a little frightened fay.
    One night, in the Fall, she runned away.

  'Out 'mong the sheep, her be,' they said,
  'Should properly have been abed;
  But sure enough she wasn't there
  Lying awake with her wide brown stare.
So over seven-acre field and up-along across the down
  We chased her, flying like a hare
  Before our lanterns. To Church-Town
    All in a shiver and a scare
  We caught her, fetched her home at last
    And turned the key upon her, fast.

She does the work about the house
As well as most, but like a mouse:
  Happy enough to chat and play
  With birds and rabbits and such as they,

农夫的新娘

夏洛蒂・缪

自相中少女，三夏飞逝，
或许太年轻——收获时，
等待更多事，或求爱。
　婚礼时，她颇害怕我，
与爱情以及人间一切事，
如同冬日，那么封闭。
她微笑出走，却不似那
　少女，更似胆怯仙子。
　　秋夜她竟逃之夭夭。

　有人说："她或在羊群，
　本该舒适地睡床榻上。"
　的确，她不在那里；
　她醒来，圆瞪着褐眼。
七亩田地，高低不平；
　追赶时，她在灯笼前，
　野兔似跑；朝教堂城，
　　一切在银辉与恐惧中。
　我们终于捉住她；将之
　　带回家并紧锁门。

她日常总做着家务活儿，
至多，真像一只小老鼠：
　只要男眷对之回避，
　少女与鸟儿、兔闲聊，

So long as men-folk keep away.
'Not near, not near!' her eyes beseech
When one of us comes within reach.
The women say that beasts in stall
Look round like children at her call.
I've hardly heard her speak at all.

Shy as a leveret, swift as he,
Straight and slight as a young larch tree,
Sweet as the first wild violets, she,
To her wild self. But what to me?

The short days shorten and the oaks are brown,
The blue smoke rises to the low grey sky,
One leaf in the still air falls slowly down,
A magpie's spotted feathers lie
At the black earth spread white with rime,
The berries redden up to Christmas-time.
What's Christmas-time without there be
Some other in the house than we!

She sleeps up in the attic there
Alone, poor maid. 'Tis but a stair
Betwixt us. Oh! my God! the down,
The soft young down of her, the brown,
The brown of her—her eyes, her hair, her hair!

　玩耍着，并分享快乐。
若有人离她近距离时，
她眼神哀求："勿走近!"
　妇女说："在她召唤下，
　圈内牲畜犹孩子张望。
　我几乎未听她说话。

她怯似野兔、快捷如飞，
似小落叶松挺拔而苗条；
野性自我：甜美似初绽：
野紫罗兰。对我为何物？

白昼苦短，橡树呈褐色；
　灰色低空，青烟袅袅，
一叶从静气流缓缓跌落。
　一喜鹊带点状的羽毛，
栖息铺白霜的黑土地上。
至圣诞节，草莓红润了。
　何为圣诞节？除我们，
　室内也无外来客哟！

　　她在阁楼上睡熟了，
　　少女孤零零；仅楼梯，
　相隔我们。上帝！下面，
　柔软茸毛；褐色、
褐色的她——明眸、乌发！

Afternoon Tea

Charlotte Mew

Please you, excuse me, good five-o'clock people,
I've lost my last hatful of words,
And my heart's in the wood up above the church steeple,
I'd rather have tea with the birds.

Gay Kate's stolen kisses, poor Barnaby's scars,
John's losses and Mary's gains,
Oh! what do they matter, my dears, to the stars
Or the glow-worms in the lanes!

I'd rather lie under the tall elm-trees,
With old rooks talking loud overhead,
To watch a red squirrel run over my knees,
Very still on my brackeny bed.

And wonder what feathers the wrens will be taking
For lining their nests next Spring;
Or why the tossed shadow of boughs in a great wind shaking
Is such a lovely thing.

下午茶

夏洛蒂·缪

请谅解吧，五点饮茶之善者，
　我失去最后仇恨的语言；
我的心，在林中教堂尖塔上，
　我宁愿与鸟儿饮茶。

快活凯特偷吻，可怜巴纳比
　伤疤，约翰所失去；玛丽
赢得。哦！何关系？亲爱的，
　飞至星辰或巷道萤火虫！

我宁愿躺在高高的榆树下方，
　听头顶上老白嘴鸦聒噪；
望着一只红松鼠，溜上膝盖，
　静静地卧于那蕨草床上。

真莫名诧异：鹪鹩衔何羽毛，
　为明春之鸟巢而铺垫？
为何飒飒树荫在大风中摇晃？
　这是多么可爱之事啊！

In the Fields

Charlotte Mew

Lord, when look at lovely things which pass,
Under old trees the shadows of young leaves
Dancing to please the wind along the grass,
Or the gold stillness of the August sun on the
August sheaves;
Can I believe there is a heavelier world than this?
And if there is
Will the strange heart of any everlasting thing
Bring me these dreams that take my breath away?
They come at evening with the home-flying rooks
and the scent of hay,
Over the fields. They come in Spring.

在田野里

夏洛蒂·缪

主啊！当我凝望美好事物经过，
　在古树下，嫩叶荫影展现时，
婆娑起舞，取悦于沿草地的
　春风，或八月金色阳光普照：
　　一束束禾梱之寂静。
我能相信天堂比之更美好吗？
　倘若真的存在，
是否有永恒之物奇异的心脏，
　将捎给我惊心动魄的梦境？
它们黄昏来临，伴着返巢白嘴鸦、
　　田野上散发的
　干草香。它们在春天来临了。

Leisure

William Davies

What is this life if, full of care,
We have no time to stand and stare;

No time to stand beneath the boughs
And stare as long as sheep or cows.

No time to see, when woods we pass,
Where squirrels hide their nuts in grass.

No time to see, in broad daylight,
Streams full of stars, like skies at night.

No time to turn at Beauty's glance,
And watch her feet, how they can dance.

No time to wait till her mouth can
Enrich that smile her eyes began.

A poor life this if, full of care,
We have no time to stand and stare.

闲　暇

威廉·戴维斯

何为生活？忧心忡忡，
我们无暇站着，凝望；

无暇站在树枝的下方，
凝目似羊群，或母牛。

无暇去看：经过树林，
松鼠在草丛里藏坚果。

无暇去看：光天化日，
溪流似夜空布满星辰。

无暇去转向美人一瞩，
观其纤足，如何舞蹈。

无暇去期待，直至她
嫣然一笑，明眸开启。

贫困生活，忧心忡忡，
我们无暇站着，凝望。

All That's Past

Walter De La Mare

Very old are the woods;
   And the buds that break
Out of the brier's boughs,
   When March winds wake,
So old with their beauty are—
   Oh, no man knows
Through what wild centuries
   Roves back the rose.

Very old are the brooks;
   And the rills that rise
Where snow sleeps cold beneath
   The azure skies
Sing such a history
   Of come and gone,
Their every drop is as wise
   As Solomon.

Very old are we men;
   Our dreams are tales
Told in dim Eden
   By Eve's nightingales;
We wake and whisper awhile,
   But, the day gone by,
Silence and sleep like fields
   Of amaranth lie.

一切都是过去

沃尔特·德·拉·梅尔

树林是多么古老!
　从那玫瑰枝上,
花蕾尽情绽放。
　三月春风醒了,
自然美如此亘古——
　哦!谁人知晓,
从那些蛮荒世纪,
　玫瑰又游回。

小河是多么古老!
　山川从沉睡的
冰雪地下高耸起。
　蔚蓝色苍穹,
咏唱这样的历史
　循环而往复;
每一颗水珠犹如
　所罗门的智慧。

人类历史很古老!
　梦境似朦胧的
伊甸园里夏娃之
　夜莺所吟故事。
我们醒来且絮语,
　而白昼逝去,
静静安眠如同那:
　田野上的紫苋。

The Listeners

Walter De La Mare

'Is there anybody there?' said the Traveller,
Knocking on the moonlit door;
And his horse in the silence champed the grasses
Of the forest's ferny floor:
And a bird flew up out of the turret,
Above the Traveller's head:
And he smote upon the door again a second time;
'Is there anybody there?' he said.
But no one descended to the Traveller;
No head from the leaf-fringed sill
Leaned over and looked into his grey eyes,
Where he stood perplexed and still.
But only a host of phantom listeners
That dwelt in the lone house then
Stood listening in the quiet of the moonlight
To that voice from the world of men:
Stood thronging the faint moonbeams on the dark stair,
That goes down to the empty hall,
Hearkening in an air stirred and shaken
By the lonely Traveller's call.
And he felt in his heart their strangeness,
Their stillness answering his cry,
While his horse moved, cropping the dark turf,
'Neath the starred and leafy sky;
For he suddenly smote on the door, even

聆听者

沃尔特·德·拉·梅尔

“家里有人吗?”旅人说道，
　敲响了月光下的房门。
万籁俱寂，马大声嚼青草，
　在森林多蕨的地面上：
一只鸟雀从塔楼飞出来，
　飞在这旅人头顶上方。
他第二次又砰砰地敲着门；
　“家里有人吗?”他说，
既无人下楼走近他身边，
　也无人从绿叶镶边的窗，
探出头，并审视其灰眼。
　他静立着，困惑不已；
而唯有一群幽灵聆听者，
　那时都住在孤寂的屋里。
他们在静谧月光下，伫立、
　聆听人类世界传来声音；
残淡月光洒满了幽暗楼梯，
　通向空荡大厅。他们伫立、
聆听孤单旅人的叫喊声，
　空气中久久回荡、摇曳。
他在心里颇觉几分怪异，
　幽灵却静静地应答呼唤。
马儿挪步，啃暗色草皮，
　灿烂星空下，枝繁叶茂。
突然他砰砰地敲门，甚至

Louder, and lifted his head: —
'Tell them I came, and no one answered,
That I kept my word,' he said.
Never the least stir made the listeners,
Though every word he spake
Fell echoing through the shadowiness of the still house
From the one man left awake:
Ay, they heard his foot upon the stirrup,
And the sound of iron on stone,
And how the silence surged softly backward,
When the plunging hoofs were gone.

更响亮了，并仰头观望——
“告之：我来了；无回音，
我是守约的，”他说道。
虽他说了每句话，聆听者
从未发出一点儿动静；
从悄悄然屋内阴影处传来，
仅留下清醒男人之回声。
啊！幽灵听见他脚踏马镫，
和石板上的铁蹄声。
马蹄猛烈前冲之声远去时，
他不知身后轻涌起寂寥。

Fare Well

Walter De La Mare

When I lie where shades of darkness
Shall no more assail mine eyes,
Nor the rain make lamentation
    When the wind sighs;
How will fare the world whose wonder
Was the very proof of me?
Memory fades, must the remembered
    Perishing be?

Oh, when this my dust surrenders
Hand, foot, lip, to dust again,
May these loved and loving faces
    Please other men!
May the rusting harvest hedgerow
Still the Traveller's Joy entwine,
And as happy children gather
    Posies once mine.

Look thy last on all things lovely,
Every hour. Let no night
Seal thy sense in deathly slumber
    Till to delight
Thou have paid thy utmost blessing;
Since that all things thou wouldst praise
Beauty took from those who loved them
    In other days.

再 见

沃尔特·德·拉·梅尔

我躺在那里，黑暗阴影，
不再困扰我的双眸，
也无雨水吟唱着悲歌，
　当风儿叹息时。
世人美好奇迹将会如何？
这即是我的明证吗？
怀念衰退，记忆之往事，
　必将磨灭吗？

哦！当我的骨灰、手足，
与唇再交付尘土时，
但愿这令人迷恋的面容，
　赢得某些男人欢心！
但愿收获的赭色灌木丛，
仍萦绕着游子欢声笑语，
好似幸福孩子采集那些——
　曾是我的花束。

珍弥最后每一时光，以及
一切美好事物。决不让
黑夜在死一般的睡眠中，
　封闭感官，直至欣欣然。
你付出了最诚挚的祝福。
既然你总是赞颂着一切，
未来，美将会来自热爱——
　他们的那些人。

The Rolling English Road

Gilbert Chesterton

Before the Roman came to Rye or out to Severn strode,
The rolling English drunkard made the rolling English road.
A reeling road, a rolling road, that rambles round the shire,
And after him the parson ran, the sexton and the squire;
A merry road, a mazy road, and such as we did tread
The night we went to Birmingham by way of Beachy Head.

I knew no harm of Bonaparte and plenty of the Squire,
And for to fight the Frenchman I did not much desire;
But I did bash their baggonets because they came arrayed
To straighten out the crooked road an English drunkard made,
Where you and I went down the lane with ale-mugs in our hands,
The night we went to Glastonbury by way of Goodwin Sands.

His sins they were forgiven him; or why do flowers run
Behind him; and the hedges all strengthening in the sun?
The wild thing went from left to right and knew not which was which,
But the wild rose was above him when they found him in the ditch.
God pardon us, nor harden us; we did not see so clear
The night we went to Bannockburn by way of Brighton Pier.

My friends, we will not go again or ape an ancient rage,
Or stretch the folly of our youth to be the shame of age,
But walk with clearer eyes and ears this path that wandereth,
And see undrugged in evening light the decent inn of death;
For there is good news yet to hear and fine things to be seen,
Before we go to Paradise by way of Kensal Green.

滚滚英格兰之路

吉伯特·切斯特顿

以前罗马人侵入莱伊，或向塞文迈进，
滚滚而来英格兰的醉汉建筑英国之路。
旋转之路、滚滚之路；在郡四周闲逛，
他身后追逐着牧师、司事和乡绅们。
快活之路、迷津之路，正如我们踏过。
夜间，我们通过滩头堡，前往伯明翰。

我知道：博那帕特和大量乡绅无危险，
我不太愿意去和那些法国人打仗。
我撞坏其袋子，因为他们却排列成队，
而拉直英格兰醉汉所修建的弯曲道路。
我与你手握啤酒杯，且沿巷道走着，
夜间，我们从古迪威桑前往格拉斯顿。

他们原谅其罪过，或为何朵朵花儿，
且追随他身后？篱笆墙在阳光下挺直？
野生物从左至右爬，不知究竟是何物？
他们发现有人卧沟渠，上方有野玫瑰。
上帝宽宥，并不冷酷；我们尚未看清，
夜间，通过布赖顿码头去了班劳伯恩。

朋友，我们不再去或模仿远古之愤怒，
或延续青春之幼稚，为年纪而羞愧；
而以清晰视听觉，走过这条蜿蜒之路。
在禁毒的夜灯下，可见体面死亡客栈；
那里可听好信息，也可见些好事情。
随后，我们通过肯萨·格林前往天堂。

The Owl

Edward Thomas

Down hill I came, hungry, and yet not starved;
Cold, yet had heat within me that was proof
Against the North wind; tired, yet so that rest
Had seemed the sweetest thing under a roof.

Then at the inn I had food, fire, and rest,
Knowing how hungry, cold, and tired was I.
All of the night was quite barred out except
An owl's cry, a most melancholy cry

Shaken out long and clear upon the hill,
No merry note, nor cause of merriment,
But one telling me plain what I escaped
And others could not, that night, as in I went.

And salted way my food, and my repose,
Salted and sobered, too, by the bird's voice
Speaking for all who lay under the stars,
Soldiers and poor, unable to rejoice.

猫头鹰

爱德华·托马斯

我下山，饥肠辘辘，尚未饿坏；
寒冷，而我内心热量，尚可以
抵御凛冽的北风。而疲劳不堪，
让人屋顶下睡眠，似乎更香甜。

在客栈，我进餐、烤火、休息；
懂得又冷又饿和疲劳的滋味。
整夜静悄悄，一切拒之门外；
除传来猫头鹰叫声，阴郁之极，

在山岭震响；声音拖长而清晰，
既无欢悦音调，也无欢悦缘由。
那晚我进屋时，有人坦率告知：
我死里逃生，别人却未能幸免。

食物和休息，已使我恢复气力；
枭声阵阵，为所有卧于星辰下：
士兵、穷人鸣不平。我沉痛，
而又清醒，却不能有点好心境。

Adlestrop

Edward Thomas

Yes, I remember Adlestrop—
The name, because one afternoon
Of heat the express-train drew up there
Unwontedly. It was late June.

The steam hissed. Someone cleared his throat.
No one left and no one came
On the bare platform. What I saw
Was Adlestrop—only the name

And willows, willow-herb, and grass,
And meadowsweet, and haycocks dry,
No whit less still and lonely fair
Than the high cloudlets in the sky.

And for that minute a blackbird sang
Close by, and round him, mistier,
Farther and farther, all the birds
Of Oxfordshire and Gloucestershire.

奥勒特普

爱德华·托马斯

是的，我记得奥勒特普——
这名字；因一下午热气
腾腾，特快火车停那里，
令人罕见。这是六月末。

蒸汽嘶嘶响。有人清嗓。
空空月台上，无人离去，
也无人来此。我所见的
即奥勒特普——唯站名、

柳树，柳树叶和青青草，
牧场香气，还有干草堆；
静寥未减几分，孤寂美，
似高高蓝天上小小云朵。

此刻，近旁乌鸫啼鸣着，
白雾缭绕；而更远之处，
更远之处，有牛津郡与
格拉斯特郡的所有鸟群。

Rain

Edward Thomas

Rain, midnight rain, nothing but the wild rain
On this bleak hut, and solitude, and me
Remembering again that I shall die
And neither hear the rain nor give it thanks
For washing me cleaner than I have been
Since I was born into this solitude.
Blessed are the dead that the rain rains upon:
But here I pray that none whom once I loved
Is dying to-night or lying still awake

Solitary, listening to the rain,
Either in pain or thus in sympathy
Helpless among the living and the dead,
Like a cold water among broken reeds,
Myriads of broken reeds all still and stiff,
Like me who have no love which this wild rain
Has not dissolved except the love of death,
If love it be for what is perfect and
Cannot, the tempest tells me, disappoint.

雨

爱德华 · 托马斯

半夜下雨，除了暴雨洗刷
我的阴湿茅屋，孑然一身。
我又记起自身即将死去，
既听不见雨声，也不感恩；
将我洗刷得比往日更洁净，
自从我诞生在孤独世界里。
祝福那些雨水淋身之死者：
我为未曾爱过之人祈祷吧！
今夜濒死，或仍清醒躺着。

我孤零零，聆听狂风暴雨，
处于痛苦中，或深深同情：
那些无助的活者，或死者，
犹冰水淹没那断裂的芦苇，
无数断苇仍静立而又僵直。
犹无爱的我，除死神之爱，
这风雨，却丝毫无动于衷。
暴风雨告诉我：倘若是爱，
必须完美，并非令人失望。

Words

Edward Thomas

Out of us all
That make rhymes,
Will you choose
Sometimes—
As the winds use
A crack in a wall
Or a drain,
Their joy or their pain
To whistle through—
Choose me,
You English words?

I know you:
You are light as dreams,
Tough as oak,
Precious as gold,
As poppies and corn,
Or an old cloak:
Sweet as our birds
To the ear,
As the burnet rose
In the heat
Of Midsummer:

Strange as the races

语　汇

爱德华·托马斯

我们外围之一切，
皆营造了节奏，
有时，你愿意
对此作出抉择吗？——
犹如风儿利用
墙上的一条缝隙，
或一道水沟。
让欢乐与悲哀，
以吹哨声而穿越——
选择我吧！
你英文之语汇？

我了解你啊！
你，即梦之光亮；
坚实似橡树，
珍贵似金子。
宛若罂粟与玉米，
或一顶旧斗篷；
宛若鸟啼声啊！
多么悦耳、甜美！
宛若地榆蔷薇，
在仲夏热气之中，
恣意而绽放！

怪异似那死亡

Of dead and unborn:
Strange and sweet
Equally,
And familiar,
To the eye,
As the dearest faces
That a man knows,
And as lost homes are:

But though older far
Than older yew, —
As our hills are, old, —
Worn new
Again and again;
Young as our streams
After rain:
And as dear
As the earth which you prove
That we love.

Make me content
With some sweetness
From Wales
Whose nightingales
Have no wings, —
From Wiltshire and Kent
And Herefordshire,
And the villages there, —
From the names, and the things
No less.

或未曾诞生种族：
怪异而又甜美，
同样地
以明眸在观赏，
颇为熟稔；
犹如男子汉知晓
恋人之姣容，
犹如失去了家园。

它远远比紫杉树，
更为古老啊！——
犹如那青山不老，
一次又一次
呈现崭新之风貌。
青春似那雨后
潺潺而流的溪水，
珍贵似那大地，
你对之已证明了
我们的爱情。

听见美妙啼声啊！
多么愉悦！
从威尔士那里，
无翼之夜莺，
传来阵阵鸣啼声——
从威尔特、肯特、
赫勒福特郡，
那里的村庄传来——
从姓氏，或更多
之轶事而传来。

Let me sometimes dance
With you,
Or climb
Or stand perchance
In ecstasy,
Fixed and free
In a rhyme,
As poets do.

让我有时与你
一起翩翩起舞吧，
或攀缘，
或偶尔欣喜若狂，
站立着；
像诗人那样
以定式或自由体，
而产生节奏感。

Overheard on a Saltmarsh

Harold Monro

Nymph, nymph,what are your beads?
Green glass, goblin.Why do you stare at them?
Give them me.
No.

Give them me. Give them me.
No.

Then I will howl all night in the reeds,
Lie in the mud and howl for them.

Goblin, why do you love them so?

They are better than stars or water,
Better than voices of winds that sing,
Better than any man's fair daughter,
Your green glass beads on a silver ring.

Hush, I stole them out of the moon.

Give me your beads, I want them.
No.

I will howl in a deep lagoon
For your green glass beads, I love them so.
Give them me. Give them.
No.

盐渍地上偶听

哈罗德·门罗

仙女，仙女，你的珠子是什么？
绿玻璃，丑妖怪，为何盯着看？
给我珠子。
不！

给我珠子，给我。
不！

那么，我将在芦苇丛整夜嗥叫；
卧在泥沼里，为珠子嗥叫。

丑妖怪，为何这么喜欢珠子？

珠子比星辰或水更为美好啊！
比风儿吟唱之声更为美妙！
比任何男人的俊女更为美丽啊！
你的绿玻璃镶嵌在一颗银戒上。

嘘！我是从月亮上偷来的珠子。

给我珠子，我多么想要啊！
不！

我将在深深的潟湖里嗥叫，
因绿色玻璃珠，我多么喜爱！
给我珠子，多么想获得啊！
不！

It Was Long Ago

Eleanor Farjeon

I'll tell you, shall I, something I remember?
Something that still means a great deal to me.
It was long ago.

A dusty road in summer I remember,
A mountain, and an old house, and a tree
That stood, you know,

Behind the house. An old woman I remember
In a red shawl with a grey cat on her knee
Humming under a tree.

She seemed the oldest thing I can remember.
But then perhaps I was not more than three.
It was long ago.

I dragged on the dusty road, and I remember
How the old woman looked over the fence at me
And seemed to know

How it felt to be three, and called out, I remember
'Do you like bilberries and cream for tea?'
I went under the tree.

And while she hummed, and the cat purred, I remember

这是很久以前

艾莉诺·法耶昂

我将告诉你，我会记得某事？
对我而言，某事仍旧余味悠长；
这是很久以前。

我记得，夏天灰蒙蒙的路，
一座高山，一栋旧宅，一棵树，
伫立着；你晓得：

在宅子后。我记得一位老太婆，
围着红披巾；膝盖上一只灰猫，
在树底下哼唱。

这似乎是我能记得最久远之事。
那时，我或许还不到三岁；
这是很久以前。

我拖曳着走在灰蒙蒙路上，记得：
老奶奶怎样从篱笆朝我张望；
她也似乎知晓：

三岁孩子如何感觉？她喊道：
“你喜欢茶里放越桔和奶酪吗？”
我走在大树下方。

她哼唱时，小猫咕噜；我记得：

How she filled a saucer with berries and cream for me
So long ago.

Such berries and such cream as I remember
I never had seen before, and never see
Today, you know.

And that is almost all I can remember,
The house, the mountain, the grey cat on her knee,
Her red shawl, and the tree,

And the taste of the berries, the feel of the sun I remember,
And the smell of everything that used to be
So long ago,

Till the heat on the road outside again I remember.
And how the long dusty road seemed to have for me
No end, you know.

That is the farthest thing I can remember.
It won't mean much to you. It does to me.
Then I grew up, you see.

她怎样用茶托装草莓和奶酪；
这是很久以前。

如此草莓！如此牛奶！我记得：
我以前从未见过；至今从未
见过；你全知晓。

这几乎是我能铭记的一切：
房宅、高山、她膝盖上的灰猫、
她的红披巾和大树、

草莓味道和阳光感触。我记得：
一切东西气味，正像往常一样；
这是很久以前。

直至路边热量又起，我记得：
漫长的灰蒙蒙路似乎使我感觉：
它无止境；你晓得。

我能记得：这是最遥远的往事。
它对你无何意义；对我却重要。
随后我长大，你明白。

The Goat Paths

James Stephens

The crooked paths go every way
Upon the hill—they wind about
Through the heather in and out
Of the quiet sunniness.
And there the goats, day after day,

Stray in sunny quietness,
Cropping here and cropping there,
As they pause and turn and pass,
Now a bit of heather spray,
Now a mouthful of the grass.

In the deeper sunniness,
In the place where nothing stirs,
Quietly in quietness,
In the quiet of the furze,
For a time they come and lie
Staring on the roving sky.

If you approach they run away,
They leap and stare, away they bound
With a sudden angry sound,
To they sunny quietude;
Crouching down where nothing stirs
In the silence of the furze,

羊肠小道

詹姆斯·斯蒂芬

山岭上，弯弯曲曲小道，
四通八达，蜿蜒而行；
于寂静的石楠丛中进出，
在和煦阳光之下。
那里山羊，一天又一天，

漫游于阳光下寂静之中，
这儿啮草，那儿啮草。
它们停留或转身或走开，
时而，吃一点石楠嫩枝，
时而，吃一口青草叶。

在阳光灿烂的更纵深处，
那里，没有什么动静，
仅一片沉寂之中的宁静。
在荆豆丛中的宁静之中，
它们一度到那里躺下，
凝视着白云飘游的天空。

若你走近，山羊会逃开，
跃起而又瞪眼，狂奔着；
对着阳光下一片沉寂，
而发出愤怒的咩咩叫声。
在荆豆丛中的宁静之中，
它们匍匐于无动静之处；

Crouching down again to brood
In the sunny solitude.

If I were as wise as they,
I would stray apart and brood,
I would beat a hidden way
Through the quiet heather spray
To a sunny solitude;

And should you come I'd run away,
I would make an angry sound,
I would stare and turn and bound
To the deeper quietude,
To the place where nothing stirs
In the silence of the furze.

In that airy quietness
I would think as long as they;
Through the quiet sunniness
I would stray away to brood
By a hidden, beaten way
In the sunny solitude

I would think until I found
Something I can never find,
Something lying on the ground,
In the bottom of my mind.

在阳光下的孤独之中，
它们匍匐着，而又沉思。

若我和小山羊同样聪明，
我会漫游离去，而沉思；
我会踏着隐蔽的小路，
穿越那静寂石楠枝条丛，
去享受灿烂阳光下孤独。

假如你来了，我会逃离，
我会发出一种愤怒吼声。
我会瞪眼、转身、狂奔，
去更为沉静的纵深处；
去那没什么动静之处，
在那荆豆丛的宁静之中。

在那空气新鲜的寂静中，
我会如同它们久久思考。
通过静寂之阳光地带，
我会漫游离开，去沉思；
踏一条隐蔽的踩平小路，
在灿烂阳光下的孤独中。

我会思考直至发现某种：
我从未能找到的东西。
那一种放在地面的某物，
它永存于我脑海之深处。

To a Poet a Thousand Years Hence

James Flecker

I who am dead a thousand years,
And wrote this sweet archaic song,
Send you my words for messengers
The way I shall not pass along.

I care not if you bridge the seas,
Or ride secure the cruel sky,
Or build consummate palaces
Of metal or of masonry.

But have you wine and music still,
And statues and a bright-eyed love,
And foolish thoughts of good and ill,
And prayers to them who sit above?

How shall we conquer? Like a wind
That falls at eve our fancies blow,
And old Maeonides the blind
Said it three thousand years ago.

O friend unseen, unborn, unknown,
Student of our sweet English tongue,
Read out my words at night, alone:
I was a poet, I was young.

Since I can never see your face,
And never shake you by the hand;
I send my soul through time and space
To greet you. You will understand.

致一千年后的诗人

詹姆斯·弗莱克

我是一个千年亡灵，
　书写甜美古风之歌；
让信使传送我话语，
　我将无法穿越此路。

不在乎你海上搭桥，
　平安驰向严寒天穹，
或建立那精美绝伦
　金属，或玉石宫殿。

你享有酒肴与音乐、
　塑像与明眸恋人吗？
善与恶之蒙昧思想，
　为位尊者祈颂祷文？

将如何征服？似狂飙，
　飘至下界。且幻想
老迈盲者：玛奥尼兹，
　三千年前即作预言。

哦！来生陌生朋友，
　学优雅英语之学子，
深夜，独诵我的诗。
　我是诗人，有朝气。

既然我们从未谋面，
　也未与君握手言欢；
我的灵魂穿越了时空，
　问候你。你将懂得。

Romance

Walter Turner

When I was but thirteen or so
　I went into a golden land,
Chimborazo, Cotopaxi
　Took me by the hand.

My father died, my brother too,
　They passed like fleeting dreams,
I stood where Popocatapetl
　In the sunlight gleams.

I dimly heard the master's voice
　And boys' far-off at play,
Chimborazo, Cotopaxi
　Had stolen me away.

I walked in a great golden dream
　To and fro from school—
Shining Popocatapetl
　The dusty streets did rule.

I walked home with a gold dark boy
　And never a word I'd say
Chimborazo, Cotopaxi
　Had taken my speech away:

浪漫传奇

沃尔特·特纳

当我约有十三岁之时，
　走进了金色大地；
钦博拉索[①]、科托帕希[②]，
　两座山牵系我的手。

父兄两人，相继离世，
　好似那飞逝之梦；
我挺立：在阳光灿烂
　波波卡特佩特山[③]。

我模糊听见师长的话，
　男孩们远远玩耍；
钦博拉索、科托帕希，
　两座山将我偷走。

我走进那金色大梦境，
　来来往往于学堂——
闪光的波波卡特佩特，
　统辖灰蒙蒙大街。

我与金冥童一起回家，
　我从来一言不发；
钦博拉索、科托帕希，
　两座山捎走我的话。

I gazed entranced upon his face
   Fairer than any flower—
O shining Popocatapetl
   It was thy magic hour:

The houses, people, traffic seemed
   Thin fading dreams by day,
Chimborazo, Cotopaxi
   They had stolen my soul away.

我出神凝望着他的脸，
　啊！胜似百花美——
闪光的波波卡特佩特，
　此是你魔幻时刻：

房宅、世人以及交通，
　似白昼渐渐残淡；
钦博拉索、科托帕希，
　两座山偷走我灵魂。

注：①钦博拉索火山：圆锥形的死火山，是厄瓜多尔最高峰。
②科托帕希火山：位于厄瓜多尔，是世界上最高的活火山。
③波波卡特佩特山：墨西哥中部雪顶上的火山，是世界上最活跃的火山之一。

Nothing to Save

David Lawrence

There is nothing to save, now all is lost,
but a tiny core of stillness in the heart
like the eyes of a violet.

无可挽救

戴维·劳伦斯

无可挽救，如今一切失落，
而心灵仅存静谧的小小内核，
似一朵紫罗兰花之眼睛。

Green

David Lawrence

The dawn was apple-green,
The sky was green wine held up in the sun,
The moon was a golden petal between.

She opened her eyes, and green
They shone, clear like flowers undone.
For the first time, now for the first time seen.

绿

戴维·劳伦斯

天宇，苹果一般的青绿，
似盛在日盘碧绿的醇酒；
月在其间，犹金色花瓣。

她睁开双眸，啊！闪烁
碧水一潭，清澈似花苞；
素昧平生，首次观赏她。

Everyone Sang

Siegfried Sassoon

Everyone suddenly burst out singing;
And I was filled with such delight
As prisoned birds must find in freedom,
Winging wildly across the white
Orchards and dark-green fields; on–on–and
out of sight.

Everyone's voice was suddenly lifted;
And beauty came like the setting sun:
My heart was shaken with tears; and horror
Drifted away... O, but Everyone
Was a bird; and the song was wordless;
the singing will never be done.

大家唱吧

希格菲德·沙逊

大家蓦然爆发响亮之歌声，
我的心田充溢如此喜悦，
似囚笼之鸟，必寻觅自由；
狂野飞翔啊！穿越白花
果园、深绿田野；飞啊飞！
　　消逝于视野里。

大家歌声蓦然高昂、激越；
美之降临似西沉之夕阳：
我的心，随泪水而颤动，
恐惧远远飘走……啊！每人
即一只鸟，唱着无言之歌；
　　歌声永远不会结束。

Amalfi[①]

Richard Aldington

We will come down to you,
O very deep sea,
And drift upon your pale green waves
Like scattered petals.

We will come down to you from the hills,
From the scented lemon-groves,
From the hot sun
We will come down.

O Thalassa[②],
And drift upon
Your pale green waves
Like petals.

注：①Amalfi：意大利城市。
②Thalassa：指海洋。

阿玛非

理查德·奥尔丁顿

我们将走进你，
哦，深深的海洋，
像散落的花瓣
漂流在苍青碧波上。

我们从山岗走近你，
从香气四溢柠檬树丛，
从炎炎太阳
走下来。

哦！深深的海洋，
我们像片片花瓣
漂流在
你苍青的碧波上。

Anthem for Doomed Youth

Wilfred Owen

What passing-bells for these who die as cattle?
—Only the monstrous anger of the guns.
—Only the stuttering rifles' rapid rattle
Can patter out their hasty orisons.
No mockeries now for them; no prayers nor bells;
Nor any voice of mourning save the choirs, —
The shrill, demented choirs of wailing shells;
And bugles calling for them from sad shires.

What candles may be held to speed them all?
Not in the hands of boys, but in their eyes
Shall shine the holy glimmers of goodbyes.
The pallor of girls' brows shall be their pall;
Their flowers the tenderness of patient minds,
And each slow dusk a drawing-down of blinds.

献给死难青年的圣歌

维尔弗雷德·欧文

什么丧钟为像牲畜般死去的人？
　——仅愤怒炮火的隆隆轰鸣声，
　——仅口吃般步枪快速咔嗒响，
才能喋喋快语着：其祈祷文。
此时不再嘲弄；无祷词、无钟声，
　也无哀悼声，除了唱诗班——
恸哭的炮弹，发狂地尖声合唱。
　在哀伤的郡县，军号召唤他们。

什么蜡烛可举起，而加速燃尽呢？
　不在士兵手里，而在其眼里，
那里闪耀着告别的神圣光辉。
　苍白少女的眉额，将是其棺罩；
他们的花卉，即宽容思想之温存。
每当迟暮黄昏时，百叶窗闭合了。

Black Monday Lovesong

Arthur Tessimond

In love's dances, in love's dances
One retreats and one advances.
One grows warmer and one colder,
One more hesitant, one bolder.
One gives what the other needed
Once, or will need, now unheeded.

One is clenched, compact, ingrowing
While the other's melting, flowing.
One is smiling and concealing
While the other's asking, kneeling.
One is arguing or sleeping
While the other's weeping, weeping.

And the question finds no answer
And the tune misleads the dancer
And the lost look finds no other
And the lost hand finds no brother
And the word is left unspoken
Till the theme and thread are broken.

When shall these divisions alter?
Echo's answer seems to falter:
'Oh the unperplexed, unvexed time
Next time ... one day ... one day ... next time!'

黑色周一情歌

亚瑟·苔西蒙德

爱情舞蹈，爱情舞蹈，
一人退步，一人向前。
一人热情，一人冷淡，
一更犹疑，一更大胆。
其中给予舞伴所欲望，
过去未来，此时忽略。

一方握拳，紧凑内延，
另一方却熔化、流淌。
一人微笑，而又隐晦，
另一人询问，并跪下。
一人争辩，或者斛然，
另一人哭泣啊！哭泣！

此问题令人难以回答，
而曲调误导着舞蹈者。
迷惘之眼无视于对方，
残疾之手触不到兄弟；
结局唯有沉默无言，
直至话题与线索中断。

何时分歧点会改变呢？
答复回声似乎很犹疑：
“哦！简单而无忧之际，
下次……一天，一天……下次！”

Not Waving but Drowning

Stevie Smith

Nobody heard him, the dead man,
But still he lay moaning:
I was much further out than you thought
And not waving but drowning.

Poor chap, he always loved larking
And now he's dead
It must have been too cold for him his heart gave way,
They said.

Oh, no no no, it was too cold always
(Still the dead one lay moaning)
I was much too far out all my life
And not waving but drowning.

不是挥手，而是淹没

斯特威·史密斯

无人听见那濒死男人，
仍旧躺着呻吟：
我远远超越你的想象，
不是挥手，而是淹没。

穷伙计，总是爱嬉耍，
此时，他死了。
这对之必定太冷酷，
他心跳停止，他们说。

哦！不！天一直太冷！
（濒死人仍躺着呻吟）：
我远离整个一生太远，
不是挥手，而是淹没。

The Sunlight on the Garden

Louis MacNeice

The sunlight on the garden
Hardens and grows cold,
We cannot cage the minute
Within its nets of gold,
When all is told
We cannot beg for pardon.

Our freedom as free lances
Advances towards its end;
The earth compels, upon it
Sonnets and birds descend;
And soon, my friend,
We shall have no time for dances.

The sky was good for flying
Defying the church bells
And every evil iron
Siren and what it tells:
The earth compels,
We are dying, Egypt, dying

And not expecting pardon,
Hardened in heart anew,
But glad to have sat under

花园中的阳光

路易斯·麦克尼斯

灿烂阳光照耀花园，
既冷酷又渐淡漠；
我们不能笼住时间，
在它的黄金之网里。
当一切告知之时，
我们不能乞求宽恕。

自由似自由之长矛，
朝向目标向前掷。
大地激发兴趣，而
商籁诗、鸟群飞降；
不久，我的朋友，
我们将无暇去跳舞。

天庭之美任鸟飞翔，
藐视教堂之鸣钟、
每一邪恶而钢铸的
海妖塞壬[①]。它告知：
大地迫使我们相信：
人濒死，埃及濒危。

切莫要期待宽恕吧，
冷酷之心已复苏；
其乐融融与你同坐——

Thunder and rain with you,
And grateful too
For sunlight on the garden.

在雷霆和暴风雨中，
也不尽感激；灿烂
阳光正照耀着花园。

注：①塞壬：半人半鸟的海妖；她常以美妙歌声诱惑海员而使得船只触礁。

Do Not Go Gentle into That Good Night

Dylan Thomas

Do not go gentle into that good night,
Old age should burn and rave at close of day;
Rage, rage against the dying of the light.

Though wise men at their end know dark is right,
Because their words had forked no lightning, they,
Do not go gentle into that good night.

Good men, the last wave by, crying how bright
Their frail deeds might have danced in a green bay,
Rage, rage against the dying of the light.

Wild men who caught and sang the sun in flight,
And learn, too late, they grieved it on its way,
Do not go gentle into that good night.

Grave men, near death, who see with blinding sight
Blind eyes could blaze like meteors and be gay,
Rage, rage against the dying of the light.

And you, my father, there on the sad height,
Curse, bless, me now with your fierce tears, I pray.
Do not go gentle into that good night.
Rage, rage against the dying of the light.

不要温文尔雅步入良宵

狄兰·托马斯

不要温文尔雅步入良宵，
暮者亡命时燃烧而又谵语；
怒斥、怒斥那光明之消亡。

智者终会知道：黑暗合理，
因他们话语无叉状之闪电；
不要温文尔雅步入良宵。

善者最后挥手，呼喊自身
微薄之力尚在绿滨上曼舞；
怒斥、怒斥那光明之消亡。

狂者抓住并歌唱飞驰太阳，
领悟太晚，哀伤行路太阳；
不要温文尔雅步入良宵。

严肃者濒死，眩然视觉中，
盲眼似流星闪光而快乐；
怒斥、怒斥那光明之消亡。

父亲于悲哀顶峰，你淌着
热泪诅咒或祝福我；我祈祷。
不要温文尔雅步入良宵。
怒斥、怒斥那光明之消亡。

Fern Hill

Dylan Thomas

Now as I was young and easy under the apple boughts
About the lilting house and happy as the grass was green,
 The night above the dingle starry,
  Time let me hail and climb
 Golden in the heydays of his eyes,
And honoured among wagons I was prince of the apple towns
And once below a time I lordly had the trees and leaves
  Trail with daisies and barley
 Down the rivers of the windfall light.

And as I was green and carefree, famous among the barns
About the happy yard and singing as the farm was home,
 In the sun that is young once only,
  Time let me play and be
 Golden in the mercy of his means,
And green and golden I was huntsman and herdsman, the calves
Sang to my horn, the foxes on the hills barked clear and cold,
  And the sabbath rang slowly
 In the pebbles of the holy streams.

All the sun long it was running, it was lovely, the hay
Fields high as the house, the tunes from the chimneys, it was air
 And playing, lovely and watery
  And fire green as grass.
 And nightly under the simple stars

蕨 山

狄兰·托马斯

我年轻时，逍遥在苹果树下，或在
房宅树影四周，快活似青草吐翠。
　在幽谷里，星光灿烂夜空中，
　　时光让我欢呼雀跃，或攀缘着
　金色年华，在其目光之下。
我簇拥于马车间，而尊为苹果城王子。
我曾卑微一时，却气派地使繁林、
　　茂叶蔓延着雏菊和大麦；
　而沿岸却是意外地降临光之河流。

我幼稚而又无忧，农庄即是家园；
我有名气，在谷仓、院落里快活歌唱。
　在太阳尚且年轻之时，
　　时光以怜悯方式，
　让我玩耍，度过那金色年华。
幼稚的金色青春里，我是猎人、牧羊人。
小牛犊随号角唱歌。山上狐狸凄清嗥叫；
　　安息日钟声缓缓地回响，
　在神圣溪流的鹅卵石上。

太阳久久迅跑，充满生机；干草田地
高似屋宇。空气从烟囱里传来曲调，
　玩耍着、生机勃勃、水汪汪的，
　　点燃着绿色如同青草。
　在纯真星辰闪烁的夜穹之下，

As I rode to sleep the owls were bearing the farm away,
All the moon long I heard, blessed among stables, the night-jars
  Flying with the ricks, and the horses
    Flashing into the dark.

And then to awake, and the farm, like a wanderer white
With the dew, come back, the cock on his shoulder: it was all
  Shining, it was Adam and maiden,
    The sky gathered again
  And the sun grew round that very day,
So it must have been after the birth of the simple light
In the first, spinning place, the spellbound horses walking warm
  Out of the whinnying green stable
    On to the fields of praise.

And honoured among foxes and pheasants by the gay house
Under the new made clouds and happy as the heart was long,
  In the sun born over and over,
    I ran my heedless ways,
  My wishes raced through the house high hay
And nothing I cared, at my sky blue trades, that time allows
In all his tuneful turning so few and such morning songs
  Before the children green and golden
    Follow him out of grace.

Nothing I cared, in the lamb white days, that time would take me
Up to the swallow thronged loft by the shadow of my hand,
  In the moon that is always rising,
    Nor that riding to sleep
  I should hear him fly with the high fields

我骑着马入睡；众夜枭夺取农庄。
我久久听月亮在马槽间祝福；夜莺
　与干草垛一起飞翔。马群儿
　　一闪而过，冲进了黑暗。

随之，我醒来；农庄如同旅人归来，
披着白露；公鸡立肩上：浑身闪光；
　这是亚当与夏娃。
　　天穹又积聚了能量，
　太阳在特殊的白昼里变圆了，
这必定在淳朴之光诞生之后吧。
世纪初旋之处，着魔之马群激烈地——
　冲出那充斥嘶叫声的绿色马槽，
　　奔驰在赞美诗一般的田地上。

快活之屋边，狐狸和野鸡礼遇我。
新生云朵下，幸福如心灵那么久远。
　太阳一次又一次诞生着，
　　我漫不经心地奔跑啊！
　我希望跑过房子和高高干草堆。
在我天穹蓝色信风里，我不在乎什么？
时光允许雅调极少转换，晨歌如此；
　在孩子稚嫩的金色年华，
　跟随着时光走出其恩典。

在羊羔纯白之日，我不在乎什么？时光
总携着我，高飞至燕子聚集的阁楼。
　在我的手阴影边，在总升起的月光下，
　　我再不会骑马而睡着了。
　我应该听见时光与高高田野在飞翔，

And wake to the farm forever fled from the childless land.
Oh as I was young and easy in the mercy of his means,
  Time held me green and dying
  Though I sang in my chains like the sea.

我醒来去农庄，逃离无童心的大地。
哦！我年轻安逸于时光之恩宠。
　虽我戴着锁链唱歌，像大海一样，
　时光却使我幼稚，而又死亡。

美国诗歌

The Death of the Flowers

William Bryant

The melancholy days are come, the saddest of the year,
Of wailing winds, and naked woods, and meadows brown and sear,
Heaped in the hollows of the grove, the autumn leaves lie dead;
They rustle to the eddying gust, and to the rabbit's tread.
The robin and the wren are flown, and from the shrubs the jay,
And from the wood-top calls the crow through all the gloomy day.

Where are the flowers, the fair young flowers, that lately sprang and stood
In brighter light and softer airs, a beauteous sisterhood?
Alas! they all are in their graves, the gentle race of flowers
Are lying in their lowly beds, with the fair and good of ours.
The rain is falling where they lie, but the cold November rain
Calls not, from out the gloomy earth the levely ones again.

The wind-flower and the violet, they perished long ago,
And the brier-rose and the orchis died, amid the summer glow;
But on the hill the goldenrod, and the aster in the wood,
And the yellow sun-flower by the brook in autumn beauty stood,
Till fell the frost from the clear cold heaven, as falls the plague on men,
And the brightness of their smile was gone, from upland, glade, and glen.

And now, when comes the calm mild day, as still such days will come,
To call the squirrel and the bee from out their winter home;
When the sound of dropping nuts is heard, though all the trees are still,
And twinkle in the smoky light the waters of the rill,

香消花殒

威廉·布赖恩特

忧郁日子即将来临，在最悲惨岁月里：
狂风怒号，树林光秃秃，草场枯黄。
秋叶死寂地匍匐，堆积于树丛坑洼里；
在飞旋飓风、野兔足迹之下簌簌作响。
知更鸟和鹪鹩飞走，樫鸟从灌丛飞走；
整个幽晦日子，乌鸦在林上呱呱叫着。

当天光璨然，空气柔润，姊妹情深时，
哪里的美丽小花新近绽放呢？
唉！温顺的百花，她们都卧于墓穴，
带着我们所称道的美丽和善良。
雨水落于她们栖身之处；十一月冷雨，
再也不会从幽冥大地上唤出美艳之花。

在炎炎夏日中，银莲花、紫罗兰久已
凋零；而多刺玫瑰和兰花也变衰败。
在明净秋色中，那山岗上金菊、林中
翠菊及小溪边黄色向阳花，亭亭玉立；
乃至清凉之苍穹降下那瘟疫般严霜，
从高地、林间、幽谷，莞然一笑而逝。

明媚白昼此刻已光临，将来还会光临；
召唤着麻雀和蜜蜂从冬巢里飞出来。
树林静悄悄，仍旧听见坚果的跌落声。
小溪的水面上闪烁着烟雾缭绕的光辉，

The south wind searches for the flowers whose fragrance late he bore,
And sighs to find them in the wood and by the stream no more.

And then I think of one who in her youthful beauty died,
The fair, meek blossom that grew up and faded by my side:
In the cold moist earth we laid her when the forest cast the leaf,
And we wept that one so lovely should have a life so brief:
Yet not unmeet it was that one, like that young friend of ours,
So gentle and so beautiful, should perish with the flowers.

南风寻觅含苞待放、新近吐芳之花卉，
声声叹息；在林里、小溪边再无芳踪。

随之，我想起她在风华正茂之时逝去，
风姿绰约花儿，在我身边花开花落。
树林落叶时她多么美艳！竟这般夭折！
我们在寒湿土地掩埋她，而为之洒泪：
然而，不仅她似一个青年友人相约，
多么温情、明丽！竟似群芳香消玉殒。

The Slave's Dream

Herry Longfellow

Beside the ungathered rice he lay,
His sickle in his hand;
His breast was bare, his matted hair
Was buried in the sand.
Again, in the mist and shadow of sleep,
He saw his Native Land.

Wide through the landscape of his dreams
The lordly Niger flowed;
Beneath the palm-trees on the plain
Once more a king he strode,
And heard the tinkling caravans
Descend the mountain road.

He saw once more his dark-eyed queen
Among her children stand;
They clasped his neck, they kissed his cheeks,
They held him by the hand!—
A tear burst from the sleeper's lids
And fell into the sand.

And then at furious speed he rode
Along the Niger's bank;
His bridle-reins were golden chains,
And, with a martial clank,

奴隶之梦

亨利·朗费罗

他躺在未收割稻子的旁边，
　手里握着镰刀；
他胸脯袒露，头发蓬乱，
　掩埋在沙地里。
在那安然入眠的阴霾之中，
　他又梦见故乡。

尼日尔河浩浩荡荡地流入：
　他梦境之风景。
在平原上的棕榈树下方，
　国王大踏步走，
再次听见那叮铛响的商队，
　从山路走下来。

他再次看见那黑眼睛女王，
　站在孩子们中央：
他们搂其颈部，吻其面颊，
　牵拉着他的手！——
泪水从安眠者眼睛里流出，
　滴落在沙地里。

随之，他以迅猛速度骑马，
　沿着尼日尔河岸；
马笼头缰绳是金色链条，
　发出威武之哐铛声。

At each leap he could feel his scabbard of steel
   Smiting his stallion's flank.

Before him, like a blood-red flag,
   The bright flamingoes flew;
From morn till night he followed their flight,
   O'er plains where the tamarind grew,
Till he saw the roofs of Caffre huts,
   And the ocean rose to view.

At night he heard the lion roar,
   And the hyena scream,
And the river-horse, as he crushed the reeds
   Beside some hidden stream;
And it passed, like a glorious roll of drums,
   Through the triumph of his dream.

The forests, with their myriad tongues,
   Shouted of liberty;
And the Blast of the Desert cried aloud,
   With a voice so wild and free,
That he started in his sleep and smiled
   At their tempestuous glee.

He did not feel the driver's whip,
   Nor the burning heat of day;
For Death had illumined the Land of Sleep,
   And his lifeless body lay
A worn-out fetter, that the soul
   Had broken and thrown away!

每一跃步，他能觉得钢鞘
　击打着战马侧翼。

他眼前飞过鲜亮的火烈鸟，
　犹如血红色旗帜；
他从早到晚跟随飞行鸟群。
　平原长满罗望子树，
直至他看见卡非人的屋顶，
　海洋景色升入视线。

夜晚，他听见一阵阵狮吼，
　与鬣狗尖叫声。
当他踩碎了芦苇丛之时，
　在隐匿的小溪旁；
河马经过，犹如鼓声雷动，
　回荡在其凯旋之梦。

层层密林以无数的舌尖儿，
　高声地呼唤自由。
沙漠上爆发着大声的呐喊，
　以狂野的自由之声。
他开始入眠，而又微笑，
　四周，暴风雨般欢乐。

他不再感觉到驱赶者皮鞭，
　也没感觉白昼炙热。
因死神照亮了“长眠大地”，
　他无生命之躯，
戴着磨旧的脚镣，而灵魂
　已破碎却又被抛弃！

The Chileren's Hour

Herry Longfellow

Between the dark and the daylight,
When the night is beginning to lower,
Comes a pause in the day's occupations,
That is known as the Children's Hour.

I hear in the chamber above me
The patter of little feet,
The sound of a door that is opened,
And voices soft and sweet.

From my study I see in the lamplight,
Descending the broad hall stair,
Grave Alice, and laughing Allegra,
And Edith with golden hair.

A whisper, and then a silence:
Yet I know by their merry eyes,
They are plotting and planning together
To take me by surprise.

A sudden rush from the stairway,
A sudden raid from the hall!
By three doors left unguarded
They enter my castle wall!

孩提时光

亨利·朗费罗

在那黑夜与日光之间，
　夜幕即降临时，
白昼忙碌之事已终止；
　这皆知孩提时光。

我听见：上方房间里，
　小脚啪哒地响，
还有打开了房门之声，
　轻柔而又安恬。

我看见：书房里灯光，
　落在大厅楼梯上；
艾丽斯稳沉，阿利拉：
　爱笑，伊迪丝金发。

喃喃细语，随之静默，
　我懂得快活眼神。
他们共同在密谋策划，
　让我出其不意。

从楼梯处，兀然冲出，
　从大厅搞突袭！
三扇门，尚未有守卫，
　他们进入城堡墙！

They climb up into my turret
　O'er the arms and back of my chair;
If I try to escape, they surround me;
　They seem to be everywhere.

They almost devour me with kisses,
　Their arms about me entwine,
Till I think of the Bishop of Bingen
　In his Mouse-Tower on the Rhine!

Do you think, O blue-eyed banditti,
　Because you have scaled the wall,
Such an old mustache as I am
　Is not a match for you all!

I have you fast in my fortress,
　And will not let you depart,
But put you down into the dungeon
　In the round-tower of my heart.

And there will I keep you forever,
　Yes, forever and a day,
Till the walls shall crumble to ruin,
　And moulder in dust away!

他们爬入小小的角楼，
爬在椅背和扶手；
我尽力逃脱，其包围
似乎无所不在。

其亲吻，几乎吞噬我，
以手臂紧紧缠绕，
直至我想起宾根主教，
在莱茵河鼠塔上！

碧眼歹徒啊！别以为：
已攀上那堵墙，
我是如此胡子拉碴的，
与你们不匹配！

我将你们拴牢在堡垒，
难以逃之夭夭，
并将之关进那处土牢，
封存我内心圆塔。

那里，我将永远珍藏；
是的，永远一天，
直至墙垣倒塌为废墟；
在尘埃中崩溃！

Barbara Frietchie

John Whittier

Up from the meadows rich with corn,
Clear in the cool September morn,

The clustered spires of Frederick stand
Green-walled by the hills of Maryland.

Round about them orchards sweep,
Apple and peach tree fruited deep,

Fair as the garden of the Lord
To the eyes of the famished rebel horde,

On that pleasant morn of the early fall
When Lee marched over the mountain-wall;

Over the mountains winding down,
Horse and foot, into Frederick town.

Forty flags with their silver stars,
Forty flags with their crimson bars,

Flapped in the morning wind: the sun
Of noon looked down, and saw not one.

Up rose old Barbara Frietchie then,

巴巴拉·费里彻

约翰·惠蒂尔

牧场上种满了丰硕谷物，
九月清晨，凉爽而清澈。

费雷德里克簇拥着尖塔，
马里兰山陵环绕着绿墙。

它们四周：果园延伸着，
苹果树、梨树果实累累。

在饥饿反叛人群的眼里，
它美丽如同上帝之花园。

在那早秋愉悦的清晨时，
“李”行走在山围墙上方；

从那高山之巅蜿蜒而下，
马蹄声声，踏进了城里。

四十面旗上，银星闪耀；
四十面旗上绛色的条纹，

在晨风中飘扬：午阳正
朝下张望，而渺无人烟。

当时，老芭芭拉站起来，

Bowed with her fourscore years ane ten;

Bravest of all in Frederick town,
She took up the flag the men hauled down;

In her attic window the staff she set,
To show that one heart was loyal yet.

Up the street came the rebel tread,
Stonewall Jackson riding ahead.

Under his slouched hat left and right
He glanced; the old flag met his sight.

'Halt!'— the dust-brown ranks stood fast.
'Fire!'— out blazed the rifle-blast.

It shivered the window, pane and sash;
It rent the banner with seam and gash.

Quick, as it fell, from the broken staff
Dame Barbara snatched the silken scarf.

She leaned far out on the window-sill,
And shook it forth with a royal will.

'Shoot, if you must, this old grey head,
But spare your country's flag,' she said.

A shade of sadness, a blush of shame.

九十岁高龄，深深鞠躬；

堪称为城里最勇敢之人，
她举起那男人拖曳之旗；

在阁楼窗上，竖起旗杆，
表明：她的心忠贞不渝。

叛军踏进街道，石墙边，
杰克逊正在骑马前行着。

他耷拉帽子，从左至右，
巡视：瞥见那眼前旧旗。

“停！”灰褐队伍迅速立正；
“开火！”步枪射击冒火焰。

这震动屋的窗框和玻璃，
并撕开旗帜裂缝与缺口。

它迅疾从断旗杆上跌落，
芭芭拉夫人猛抓起丝巾；

将身子远远地探出窗口，
以崇高意志向前摆动着。

“你必须射击我的灰脑袋，
而留下你们国家的旗帜。”

悲哀之阴影、满目之羞愧，

Over the face of the leader came;

The nobler nature within him stirred
To life at that woman's deed and word;

'Who touches a hair of yon gray head
Dies like a dog! March on!' he said.

All day long through Frederick street
Sounded the tread of marching feet:

All day long that free flag tost
Over the heads of the rebel host.

Ever its torn folds rose and fell
On the loyal winds that loved it well;

And through the hill-gaps sunset light
Shone over it with a warm good-night.

Barbara Frietchie's work is o'er,
And the Rebel rides on his raids no more.

Honor to her! and let a tear
Fall, for her sake, on Stonewall's bier.

Over Barbara Frietchie's grave,
Flag of Freedom and Union, wave!

Peace and order and beauty draw

却显现在这头目的脸上。

老妇人行为和铮铮话语，
激活他内心高尚的天性。

“谁敢碰她一根灰色头发，
狗一样死去！前进！”他说。

整天通过费雷德里克街，
行军脚步踩踏声又响起。

整天，自由旗帜飘动于——
叛乱军队的头顶之上方；

撕坏的旗褶在上下飘拂，
在热爱它的忠诚之风中。

通过山隘口，落日之光
映照上方，热情道晚安。

芭芭拉的工作已经完毕，
叛军再也不骑马来袭击。

向她致敬！为了她缘故，
泪水抛洒在石墙棺材上。

在老芭芭拉的坟墓之上，
自由、团结旗帜在飘舞！

和平、秩序和美丽吸引

Round thy symbol of light and law;

And ever the stars above look down
On thy stars below in Frederick town!

在光明、法律象征周围。

天上星辰永远朝下张望：
人间星辰在费雷德里克！

Tell All the Truth

Emily Dickinson

Tell all the Truth but tell it slant—
Success in Circuit lies
Too bright for our infirm Delight
The Truths superb surprise
As Lightning to the Children eased
With explanation kind
The Truth must dazzle gradually
Or every man be blind—

告知一切真理

艾米莉·狄更森

告知真理，却告知观点——
电路成功在于太明亮，
却为我们捎来少许欢乐。
真理之壮丽似闪电一般，
使孩子们惊骇；且加以
好言安慰，并给予解释。
真理之光，令人渐眩目，
否则每个男人将成盲者。

Acquainted with the Night

Robert Frost

I have been one acquainted with the night.
I have walked out in rain—and back in rain.
I have outwalked the furthest city light.

I have looked down the saddest city lane.
I have passed by the watchman on his beat
And dropped my eyes, unwilling to explain.

I have stood still and stopped the sound of feet
When far away an interrupted cry
Came over houses from another street,

But not to call me back or say good-by;
And further still at an unearthly height,
One luminary clock against the sky

Proclaimed the time was neither wrong nor right.
I have been one acquainted with the night.

熟悉黑夜

罗伯特・弗洛斯特

我一直是熟悉黑夜之人，
从雨里走出——从雨里走回。
我超越最远的城市灯光。

我俯瞰最悲哀的城市巷道。
我经过正巡逻的打更夫，
我垂下眼睛，不愿意解释。

我静立着，而停下脚步声。
当远处突如其来的叫喊声，
从另一条街道的房宅传来：

不是召我回去或说声再见。
更远处，在非尘世之高度，
一只发光之钟映衬着苍穹；

报导时间既不错，也不对。
因我一直是熟悉黑夜之人。

After Apple Picking

Robert Frost

My long two-pointed ladder's sticking through a tree
Toward heaven still,
And there's a barrel that I didn't fill
Beside it, and there may be two or three
Apples I didn't pick upon some bough.
But I am done with apple-picking now.
Essence of winter sleep is on the night,
The scent of apples: I am drowsing off.
I cannot rub the strangeness from my sight—
I got from looking through a pane of glass,
I skimmed this morning from the drinking trough,
And held against the world of hoary grass.
It melted, and I let it fall and break.
But I was well
Upon my way to sleep before it fell,
And I could tell
What form my dreaming was about to take.
Magnified apples appear and disappear,
Stem end and blossom end,
And every fleck of russet showing clear.
My instep arch not only keeps the ache,
It keeps the pressure of a ladder-round.
I feel the ladder sway as the boughs bend.
And I keep hearing from the cellar bin
The rumbling sound

采摘苹果之后

罗伯特 · 弗洛斯特

两根立柱的长梯紧紧靠在树上，
仍朝上指着天空，
尚有一桶我未装满。
它旁边，或许一些果枝上，
留有两三个苹果未采摘。
此时，我已忙完活儿，
冬眠的精髓在于夜间时辰；
苹果香味渐渐地催我入眠。
我难以从视线里抹去那——
透过一块玻璃所见的奇观。
今晨，我从饮水槽边掠过，
并以此与衰草世界相比。
它消融；我使之降临、中断。
梦境来临前，我睡得正香。
我可以告诉：
我的梦将以什么方式呈现：
苹果放大了，出现又消失，
在枝干末端与花梢上，
赤褐苹果上每个斑点很清晰。
我拱起的脚背不仅持续疼痛，
还承受梯子四周树枝的压力。
枝条弯下，只觉梯子摇晃；
我一直听见地窖贮藏室里的
轱辘响声：

Of load on load of apples coming in.
For I have had too much
Of apple-picking: I am overtired
Of the great harvest I myself desired.
There were ten thousand thousand fruit to touch,
Cherish in hand, lift down, and not let fall.
For all
That struck the earth,
No matter if not bruised or spiked with stubble,
Went surely to the cider-apple heap
As of no worth.
One can see what will trouble
This sleep of mine, whatever sleep it is.
Were he not gone,
The woodchuck could say whether it's like his
Long sleep, as I describe its coming on,
Or just some human sleep.

运进了一担又一担苹果。
因我已采摘
大量苹果，而过度劳累了；
因本人奢望有丰硕收成。
我必须触摸成千上万的果实，
我爱不释手，抬下来以免
摔坏了。因为所有的——
碰到地面上的苹果，
不管碰伤与否，或粘上残枝，
无疑，一概扔至酿酒苹果堆，
作为一些贬值物。
人们可能会明白：什么打扰
我的睡眠，无论我睡得如何？
若他尚未离去，
土拨鼠会说：是否如同他
漫长冬眠？正如我所描述：
它来临了，正如某人安眠。

The Tuft of Flowers

Robert Frost

I went to turn the grass once after one
Who mowed it in the dew before the sun.

The dew was gone that made his blade so keen
Before I came to view the levelled scene.

I looked for him behind an isle of trees;
I listened for his whetstone on the breeze.

But he had gone his way, the grass all mown,
And I must be, as he had been,—alone,

'As all must be,' I said within my heart,
'Whether they work together or apart.'

But as I said it, swift there passed me by
On noiseless wing a 'wildered butterfly,

Seeking with memories grown dim o'er night
Some resting flower of yesterday's delight.

And once I marked his flight go round and round,
As where some flower lay withering on the ground.

And then he flew as far as eye could see,

一簇花

罗伯特·弗罗斯特

日出前，他在露水地刈草；
随之，我再前往翻动青草。

露珠消失，草叶更香气袭人；
随之，我去欣赏平整的场地。

在绿树的岛屿，我寻访他；
在微风中，我倾听磨石声。

他已动身走了，草全刈完；
我必然似他那般——孤单。

“必然如此，”我倾吐心语，
“无论他们劳作或分离。”

我话音未落，迷茫的蝴蝶，
无声之翼从身边疾驶而过，

带着在黑夜变阴晦的记忆；
寻觅昨日愉悦的凋谢之花。

我凝视蝶儿到处飞来飞去，
好似花儿枯萎而遗弃地上；

然后，飞至我的极目之处，

And then on tremulous wing came back to me.

I thought of questions that have no reply,
And would have turned to toss the grass to dry;

But he turned first, and led my eye to look
At a tall tuft of flowers beside a brook,

A leaping tongue of bloom the scythe had spared
Beside a reedy brook the scythe had bared.

I left my place to know them by their name,
Finding them butterfly weed when I came.

The mower in the dew had loved them thus,
By leaving them to flourish, not for us,

Nor yet to draw one thought of ours to him.
But from sheer morning gladness at the brim.

The butterfly and I had lit upon,
Nevertheless, a message from the dawn,

That made me hear the wakening birds around,
And hear his long scythe whispering to the ground,

And feel a spirit kindred to my own;
So that henceforth I worked no more alone;

But glad with him, I worked as with his aid,

再飞回我身旁，翅翼抖怵。

我寻思着苦无答案的问题，
并把青草翻动，颠簸而晾干。

蝶始先回转，引人注目那
匍匐在小溪边硕大的花簇。

溪流芦苇丛生，长镰已钝，
幸而留下跃动舌状的花朵。

我离开原处，而前去观赏，
这才知晓：蝴蝶花之名称。

露水地刈割者，如此爱花，
让其繁茂生长而不为我们，

也不让我们思绪接近于他；
仅从边缘获得纯粹之晨乐。

然而，我和这一只蝴蝶儿，
却从黎明，偶得一点信息，

使我听见醒来的鸟儿盘旋，
听见他的长镰对大地絮语，

觉得灵感点燃了我的心灵；
从此，我的劳作不再孤寂。

我欢愉地得到了他的协助，

And weary, sought at noon with him the shade;

And dreaming, as it were, held brotherly speech
With one whose thought I had not hoped to reach.

'Men work together,' I told him from the heart,
'Whether they work together or apart.'

疲乏时与之去午间的树荫；

梦幻一如既往兄弟般谈心，
其思想，我真是难以企及。

“人类共同劳作”，我诉心语，
“无论他们一起劳作或分离。”

Dawn

William Carlos Williams

Ecstatic birds songs pound
the hollow vastness of the sky
with metallic clinkings—
heating color up into it
at a far edge,—beating it,beating it
with rising, triumphant ardor,—
stirring it into warmth,
quickening in it a spreading change,—
bursting wildly against it as
dividing the horizon, a heaven sun
lifts himself—is lifted—
bit by bit above the edge
of things,—runs free at last
out into the open—! lumbering
glorified in full release upward—
songs cease.

晨 曦

威廉·卡洛斯·威廉斯

狂喜的鸟啼声，砰砰地
敲击空旷而广袤的苍穹，
带着金属般的铿锵声——
将五彩缤纷敲进遥远天宇。
浩渺的边缘——敲呀，敲！
带着高涨的胜利狂欢——
鼓动起天穹的激情，
加速其蔓延铺展之变化——
沉重日盘自行举起——
上升——狂野地冲出天际，
平分地平线，冉冉上升
至穹顶——最后自由迅跑
在广阔空间——笨重躯体
颂扬着全部向上的释放——
　　　　鸟啼已停。

Fire Spirit

William Carlos Williams

I am old.
You warm yourselves at these fire?
In the center of these flames
I sit, my teeth chatter!
Where shall I turn for comfort?

火的精神

威廉·卡洛斯·威廉斯

我老了。
你们在火炉边取暖吗?
在一团团火焰的中央,
我端坐,牙齿打颤,
哪里我将会寻到安乐?

Peace on the Earth

William Carlos Williams

The Archer is wake!
The Swan is flying!
Gold against blue
An Arrow is lying.
There is hunting in heaven—
Sleep safe till tomorrow.

The Bears are aboard!
The Eagle is screaming!
Gold against blue
The eyes are gleaming!
Sleep!
Sleep safe till tomorrow.

The Sisters lie
With their arms intertwining;
Gold against blue
Their hair is shining!
The Serpent writhes!
Orion is listening!
Gold against blue
His sword is glistening!
Sleep!
There is hunting in heaven—
Sleep safe till tomorrow.

地球上的太平

威廉·卡洛斯·威廉斯

人马座已醒来！
天鹅座在飞翔！
金光映衬蓝色天光，
一支箭在躺着。
天穹展开一场狩猎——
安然睡去直至天明。

众熊座在出游！
天鹰座在尖叫！
金光映衬蓝色天光，
其目光熠熠生辉！
安睡吧！
安然睡去直至天明。

昴星团七姊妹却
手挽手地安卧着；
金光映衬蓝色天光，
她们的秀发在闪烁！
巨蛇座在扭动！
猎户座在恭听！
金光映衬蓝色天光，
他的利剑反射光芒！
安睡吧！
天穹展开一场狩猎——
安然睡去直至天明。

To Mark Anthony in Heaven

William Carlos Williams

This quiet morning light
Reflected, how many times
From grass and trees and clouds
Enters my north room,
Touching the walls with
Grass and clouds and trees.
Anthony,
Trees and grass and clouds.
Why did you follow
that beloved body
With your ships at Actium?
I hope it was because
You know her inch by inch
From slanting feet upward
To the roots of her hair
And down again and that you saw her
Above the battle's fury—
Clouds and trees and grass—

For then you are
listening in heaven.

仰望天上安东尼

威廉·卡洛斯·威廉斯

这静穆的晨曦啊！
闪烁着，多少次
从草地、树林、云层
照进我的北厢房。
草儿、云儿、树儿
拂动着墙垣。
安东尼，
树儿、草儿、云儿。
为何你在阿克蒂姆，
乘着战舰追随着
那光彩照人的身躯呢？
我希冀：这因为
你完全地熟悉她啊！
从她倾斜的纤足
上至秀发末梢。
在下方，你又会看见
她高耸于愤怒的——
战云、树林、草地上——

因为你那时正在
天穹上聆听着。

The Return

Ezra Pound

See, they return; ah, see the tentative
Movements, and the slow feet,
The trouble in the pace and the uncertain
Wavering!
See, they return, one, and by one,
With fear, as half-awakened;
As if the snow should hesitate
And murmur in the wind,
                and half turn back;
These were the "Wing'd-with-Awe",
                            Inviolable.
Gods of the wingèd shoe!
With them the silver hounds,
                sniffing the trace of air!

Haie! Haie!
              These were the swift to harry;
These the keen-scented;
These were the souls of blood.

Slow on the leash,
       pallid the leash-men!

归　来

埃兹拉·庞德

瞧，他们归来；啊！看踌躇的
动作，缓缓的脚步，
步履中的忧虑，不平稳地
摇曳！
看，他们归来，一个接一个，
带着恐惧，揉着惺忪的睡眼；
犹如白雪在踌躇，
在风中絮语，
　　　走了一半的归途。
这些是“令人敬畏的天使”，
　　　　　　不可亵渎。
天使脚下插着飞翼！
银色猎犬跟随他们，
　　　　嗅着空气的踪迹！

哎呀！哎呀！
　　　这就是雨燕的侵扰；
这就是嗅觉敏锐的人；
这就是有血有肉的灵魂。

慢慢在皮带下挣扎，
　　　苍白的被羁绊的人！

Dirge Without Music

Edna Millay

I am not resigned to the shutting away of loving hearts in the
hard ground.
So it is, and so it will be, for so it has been, time out of
mind:
Into the darkness they go, the wise and the lovely. Crowned
With lilies and with laurel they go; but I am not resigned.
Lovers and thinkers, into the earth with you.
Be one with the dull, the indiscriminate dust.
A fragment of what you felt, of what you knew,
A formula, a phrase remains, —but the best is lost.

The answers quick and keen, the honest look, the laughter,
the love,—
They are gone. They are gone to feed the roses. Elegant and
curled
Is the blossom. Fragrant is the blossom. I know. But I do not
approve.
More precious was the light in your eyes than all the roses
in the world.

Gently they go, the beautiful, the tender, the kind;
Quietly they go, the intelligent, the witty, the brave.
I know. But I do not approve. And I am not resigned.

无音乐的挽歌

艾德拉·米莱

苦难大地上，我不会放弃去关闭
那爱情心窗。
现在如此，将来如此；因一直如此
而忘记时间。
他们走进了黑暗，聪颖而又可爱。
他们走了，头戴着百合花和桂冠；
而我不愿放弃。
你与情侣和思想家走进了大地，
却与无可选择的黯淡尘土而相伴。
你感觉之碎片，你认知之碎片，
某定式和片语仍保存——最好却失去。

回答既迅速又尖锐，诚实目光、
朗朗笑声、爱情——
他们逝去化春泥滋养玫瑰。花儿
优雅、卷曲地盛开；花儿芬芳四溢。
我知晓，却不赞同。
你目光明辉远比世界上一切玫瑰花，
更为令人珍弥啊！

他们轻轻走了，美丽、温柔而又善良。
他们静静走了，聪颖、机智而又勇敢。
我知晓，既不表示赞同，也不会放弃。

Sonnet

Edna Millay

Time does not bring relief; you all have lied
Who told me time would ease me of my pain!
I miss him in the weeping of the rain;
I want him at the shrinking of the tide;
The old snows melt from every mountain-side,
And last year's leaves are smoke in every lane;
But last year's bitter loving must remain
Heaped on my heart, and my old thoughts abide.
There are a hundred places where I fear
To go, —so with his memory they brim.
And entering with relief some quiet place
Where never fell his foot or shone his face,
I say, 'There is no memory of him here!'
And so stand stricken, so remembering him.

商籁诗

艾德拉 · 米莱

时间未有慰藉；你们撒谎，
告诉我：时间会减轻痛苦！
在泪水滂沱中，我思念他；
在潮汐衰落时，我想见他。
每一山崖千古冰雪会消融，
每一巷道枯叶已化为烟云。
往年苦恋必然一如既往而
堆积心房；昔时情思绵绵。
那里百余之处，我真惶然
前往——因充溢他的记忆。
我颇释怀地走入静谧之处，
再无他足音与灿烂之笑容。
我说："这里消失其记忆！"
如此承受打击，如此缅怀！

Somewhere I Have Never Travelled

Edward Cummings

somewhere i have never travelled, gladly beyond
any experience, your eyes have their silence:
in your most frail gesture are things which enclose me,
or which i cannot touch because they are too near

your slightest look easily will unclose me
though i have closed myself as fingers,
you open always petal by petal myself as Spring opens
(touching skilfully, mysteriously) her first rose

or if your wish be to close me, i and
my life will shut very beautifully, suddenly,
as when the heart of this flower imagines
the snow carefully everywhere descending;

nothing which we are to perceive in this world equals
the power of your intense fragility: whose texture
compels me with the colour of its countries,
rendering death and forever with each breathing

(i do not know what it is about you that closes
and opens; only something in me understands
the voice of your eyes is deeper than all roses)
nobody, not even the rain, has such small hands

我从未漫游某处

爱德华·肯明斯

我从未漫游某处，快乐超越
任何经历，你明眸蕴含沉默：
娇柔不堪姿态将会封闭我，
或我难以触摸，因其太近于

你微妙目光，易打开我心扉。
虽我似纤纤手指关闭自我，
你总将我一瓣瓣打开，似春天
初绽玫瑰（娴熟神秘地轻抚）。

若你想接近，我与个人生活，
将会关闭，优美而又蓦然，
好似此花蕊展开那想象之力：
雪花每一处小心翼翼地飘落。

我们感知世上无物可等同于——
你极其微弱之力：谁之纹理，
却迫使我染就乡土之色彩？
给予死亡，永伴着每次呼吸。

（我不知你四周何物在开合着。
仅有我内心某种感知能理解：
你目光里声音比玫瑰更深沉。）
谁有如此纤细之手，甚至雨水。

Puzzled

Langston Hughes

Here on the edge of hell
Stands Harlem—
Remembering the old lies,
The old kicks in the back,
The old, *Be patient*,
They told us before.

Sure, we remember.
Now, when the man at the corner store
Says sugar's gone up another two cents,
And bread one,
And there's a new tax on cigarettes—
We remember the job we never had,
Never could get,
And can't have now
Because we're colored.

So we stand here
On the edge of hell
In Harlem
And look out on the world
And wonder
What we're gonna do
In the face of what
We remember.

困　惑

兰斯顿 · 休斯

这里，在地狱边缘上，
耸立着哈莱姆——
铭记这古老谎言、
背部上久远之踢痕；
先民，忍耐吧！
他们过去告诉了我们。

的确，我们已记住。
现在，街角商店人，
说糖又长价了二美分。
面包一美分，
还有香烟又加新税——
我们记得：从未工作，
永远不可能得到。
而此时，也不能拥有，
因我们是有色人种。

故而，我们立于此，
在地狱之边缘上。
在哈莱姆，
放眼遥望着整个世界，
并奇怪：
我们将会做什么？
面临着我们：
所铭记住的那一切。

The Dream

Theodore Roethke

1

I met her as a blossom on a stem
Before she ever breathed, and in that dream
The mind remembers from a deeper sleep:
Eye learned from eye, cold lip from sensual lip.
My dream divided on a point fire;
Light hardened on the water where we were;
A bird sang low; the moonlight sift in;
The water rippled,and she rippled on.

2

She came toward me in the flowing air,
A shape of change, encircled by its fire.
I watched her there, between me and the moon;
The bushes and stones danced on and on;
I touched her shadow when the light delayed;
I turned my face away, and yet she stayed.
A bird sang from the center of a tree;
She loved the wind because the wind loved me.

3

Love is not love until love's vulnerable.
She slowed to sigh, in that long interval.
A small bird flew in circles where we stood,
the deer came down, out of the dappled wood.

梦 境

西奥多 · 罗特克

1

她曾鲜活着，我遇见着她，
似花儿绽放枝头。在梦境，
大脑从沉睡之中唤起记忆：
从目光知晓性感之唇冰冷。
我的梦在火焰尖端上切割，
我们停留水面上，光凝结。
一只鸟浅唱，而月光泻进；
水波潋滟，她随波飘动着。

2

在飞旋气流中她姗姗而来，
一团火焰环绕变幻之身影；
我凝视：她在我与明月间。
灌木丛与岩石，翩翩起舞；
光之游移之中我触摸阴影，
我转过脸庞，而她却流连。
她爱恋风儿，因风爱恋我。

3

爱神并非爱情直至爱受伤。
悠长间歇中，她缓步叹息。
小鸟飞旋进我们伫立之处；
鹿儿从斑驳之林里奔出；

All who remember, doubt. Who calls that strange?
I tossed a stone, and listened to its plunge.
She knew the grammer of least motion,
She lent me one virtue and I live thereby.

4

She held her body steady in the wind;
Our shadows met, and slowly swung around;
She turned the field into a glittering sea;
I played in flame and water like a boy
And I swayed out beyond the white seafoam;
Like a wet log, I sang within a flame.
In that last while, eternity's confine,
I came to love, I came into my own.

记忆之人怀疑。谁称怪异？
我晃动岩石，听其下跌声。
她却知晓：最小运动法则；
赐一种美德，我由此生存。

4

她在风之中，使身体平稳；
我们的影子相拥，旋转着，
她将田地转之为一片光海。
我似男孩在火与水中玩耍，
我在海浪白沫之中摇摆着，
似一块湿木在火焰里歌唱。
在最终时辰，永恒之境界，
我走向恋人，也走进自我。